HACKER'S ACCOMPLICE

HUNT SECURITY, BOOK 2

JASMINE C. CALDWELL

Content Warnings

**Every criminal has a line they won't cross.
Frankie just found hers.**

When Frankie, also known as the infamous hacker Eraser X, discovers her employer has been running a trafficking ring, she doesn't just get out: she vows to take them down. She runs to an old friend to help rescue the victims and put an end to the criminal syndicate. But when she arrives, she discovers even more allies, including the devastatingly handsome Sam.

Sam, a burned out FBI agent, is on a much-needed vacation when Frankie shows up at his best friend's house. She wants help to take down a human trafficking group, and he's all in. But he doesn't realize that Frankie used to work for the bad guys. Not until he realizes that Frankie's signature is the same as the hacker he's spent months trying to find.

How can he turn Frankie in when she holds his heart? But someone has to answer for her crimes...

Prologue

She'd just about worked the buckle out of the car seat when the vehicle came to a stop. "We're here," said the lady with the graying hair. Miss Lisa had deep skin like Frankie, and she was really tall. She was always nice, but Frankie didn't trust her.

She'd been the one to convince her to leave when Mommy fell on the floor and didn't get up.

The family she'd been living with had a nice house, and a swing set in the backyard. But Miss Lisa had grabbed all her things and brought her to another house. Was this where Mommy was? Surely Mommy was awake by now. It had been... Frankie wasn't sure how long it had been since she'd seen her mom, but it had been spring when she went to live with the Clemenses and it was almost Halloween. Greg and Violet Clemens had been talking about Halloween and trick-or-treating, which Frankie hadn't understood. When they explained that you got candy, Frankie was all in.

But then the Clemenses had started boxing all their stuff. Mister Clemens had apparently got a new job in a place called Idaho. And then Miss Lisa came for her.

This house was short, and close to other houses that looked just like it. Instead of a hard driveway, this one was filled with small gray stones. How was she supposed to draw with chalk on this?

Miss Lisa reached into the back of the car and clucked her tongue. "Now, Francesca. We don't unbuckle ourselves when the car is moving."

Frankie just stared. It always unnerved the grown-ups when she did that. All of them except Miss Lisa, it seemed.

Her feet landed on the funny driveway and Miss Lisa took her by the hand. They walked up three steps and Miss Lisa knocked on the storm door. The inside door opened first, then the outer one.

"Hello there, Miss Lisa. And who have you brought us?" A pale lady with greasy dark hair looked down at her.

"Aubrey, this is Francesca." Miss Lisa turned to Frankie and kneeled down. "You're going to stay with Aubrey and her family now."

Frankie scowled. No one had said anything, but she'd thought when Miss Lisa came for her it would be to take her back to her mother. "Want Mommy."

"I'm sorry, sweetie, but Mommy is in Heaven."

So then take me there! But Frankie couldn't verbalize that yet. Instead, she stomped her foot and crossed her arms over her chest.

"We're happy for you to stay with us, Francesca."

Ugh, this again. She glared up at this Aubrey person. "Me Fwankie."

Miss Lisa stood when Aubrey looked confused. "According to the previous foster parents, she prefers to go by Frankie."

"You said she was four, right?" The pale lady chewed on something in her mouth.

"Yes, but her speech patterns seem to be delayed. It's not uncommon in her situation. She has speech therapy every Friday at two. The information is in her file." Miss Lisa passed a folder over to Aubrey, who thumbed through it.

"Well, I'll get her stuff out of the car."

Aubrey took her hand and led her inside. "Do you like *Blue's Clues*?"

Frankie shrugged. Aubrey turned the television on, and a blue dog distracted Frankie from her new life.

After Miss Lisa said goodbye, Miss Aubrey left the TV on and was reading a book at the kitchen table. Frankie took it upon herself to search for her mom herself. She wandered up to the other end of the small house, but all she found were a couple of bedrooms and a bathroom.

The door slammed shut and a male voice yelled. "Aubrey, why is that godforsaken show on again? You know I hate that shit."

"Oh, my God! I told you Lisa was dropping off a kid today. She's four. I put it on for her."

"I don't see no kid. And ours are too old for that." The loud voices made Frankie's tummy feel funny, and she slipped into the dark bathroom to hide.

"She was there a second ago! Frankie, sweetie, where did you go? Come meet Mister Rob."

It didn't take Miss Aubrey long to locate her where she was trying to hide behind the potty.

"Johnny and Sarah will be home from school soon. Sarah has the pink room. You're going to share with her. I bet you'll be great friends."

Frankie wasn't so sure. The pink bedroom hadn't had any toys, just a lot of furniture.

She sat Frankie in front of the TV again with that boring blue dog, and Frankie laid her head down, defeated. Mommy wasn't here, either. Where was Heaven, and why couldn't Mommy come back?

FRANKIE, AGE 20

"Did one of you assholes eat my sandwich?" Frankie Davis shouted as she slammed the refrigerator door shut. The video game noises in the background just got louder. Why the hell did she even bother asking when she knew no one would own up to the theft?

A quick peek in the garbage can showed the empty Styrofoam that once held her leftovers. Damn it, now she'd have to hit the soup kitchen for lunch. They didn't have any groceries to speak of. Frankie sure as hell never bought any. Not only had she never learned how to cook, she couldn't trust her roommates not to eat her food.

She marched past the living room of the tiny two-bedroom apartment she shared with three other people, Victor's game on in the background. If her lousy roommates had any money, she'd just siphon off the cost of the sandwich from their accounts. She could transfer some of her cryptocurrency, but not in time for her to deal with her empty stomach.

None of them had much. They'd dropped out of school during their time in the group home and most honest jobs required at least a GED. So they took whatever work they could get. Victor ran deliveries for the dealer on the corner. Maverick picked pockets or stole hub caps and sold his goods to the pawnshop. Sharon turned tricks and practiced stripping in her spare time to hopefully get a job as a dancer. And Frankie used the computer. But still, to eat her sandwich?

"Hey Frankie, can you pick up—"

"Fuck off." She gave him the finger as she slammed the front door so hard the chain rattled.

She'd been looking forward to the rest of her Italian hoagie all morning, one of the few indulgences she allowed herself. And the assholes had eaten it. Her name had been on the container. Damn it!

Too bad Victor's ancient gaming console wasn't worth anything. She could have stolen it and sold it as payback. But her sandwich was worth more than a beat-up, barely-plays-anything PlayStation 3. She'd looked up the value online. Besides, Victor locked it away when he wasn't playing it. None of them trusted the others any further than they could throw them.

Fuming, she strode down the sidewalk, people dodging out of her way. This was ridiculous. Frankie needed her *own* space.

She made it to the soup kitchen in record time, but there was still a line out the door. Resigned, she crossed her arms over her chest and leaned against the wall, waiting to move forward.

One nice thing about coming to the soup kitchen was the free wi-fi. Frankie pulled out her ancient, battered cell phone that she'd bought from the pawnshop and pulled up her email.

Along with the usual junk cluttering her inbox, was a subject line that gave her pause. *You have a private message on LiteByte Zone.* LBZ was a coding forum. They didn't bother to monitor the private groups, so that's where Frankie had learned her trade.

Curious, she opened the email.

Dear Eraser X,

We have a job for someone with your unique skill set. The pay is competitive, and we promise absolute discretion. Your assignment would entail locating a document in a particular server and deleting it.

Her eyes about popped out of her head when she saw the pay they listed.

> **If this arrangement works out, we can provide you with more jobs like this one, for even more money. Please reply with a private email address for more information.**

Hot damn! All of Frankie's problems would be solved. She wouldn't have to steal credit card numbers and make fake cards anymore. Those only got you so far until people figured it out and the bank shut the card down. And most people knew how to spot a phishing scam these days.

She was always careful not to leave a trace. Hence the name, Eraser.

As the line moved forward, Frankie frantically typed out a reply. She'd see where this went. Maybe this was her ticket out.

Chapter 1

"Fox did *what*?" Frankie said over the encrypted line.

"She's turned against us, Eraser. We need your help. We're going to... send a message. I want Fox to come back."

Now that she thought about it, Fox had been silent for quite a while, which Frankie had been curious about. She figured maybe she was taking a break from jewel heists, or even working with a different hacker to get into the museums she was infamous for stealing from. But to hear that Fox had turned state's evidence?

It was like a knife in the gut.

"What do you need from me?" While Frankie didn't care much for her boss and contact at the syndicate, Larry, the syndicate had made her good money. It just sucked sometimes that everything came through him.

"I need you to look into her bodyguard and the address we have for her. I want to be sure there are no cameras at this apartment. Sandstorm and Gambit are going in while she's at work tonight."

"Alright. Send me the info."

"Done. Gambit and Sandstorm will contact you at five your time."

"Got it." Frankie shook her head as she hung up the VOIP call with her boss.

How could the Sly Fox have turned on them like this? They'd worked together for years. She'd been Fox's invisibility cloak, and she'd thought they were friends. At least, as close to friends as they could get in the syndicate. But just like everyone else, Fox had left her. This was exactly why she didn't let anyone get close.

Frankie eyed the clock and got to work. She had three hours to get the lay of the land.

Baltimore, huh? Her former colleague had certainly gotten far. You couldn't get much further from Las Vegas without taking a boat. And whoever Foxy hired as a bodyguard had never known a hacker. His camera system might be top of the line, but that just made it slightly more difficult to crack. And Eraser was the best.

Once she knew what she was doing, she sat back with a book until five o'clock rolled around. The buzz in her headset alerted her to Gambit and Sandstorm signing into the syndicate server. Foxy had been willing to use her private server, but she didn't know Gambit and Sandstorm that well to give them a direct line to her that even Larry didn't have.

"Yo, Eraser. We parked the car. Can you get the cameras turned off?"

She had to roll her eyes at these stupid white boys. "If you want the bodyguard to know exactly when you were there, sure."

"Come on, bitch, don't make this any harder."

"Excuse you? Remember who's covering your asses, boys."

"Shut up, moron." At least one of them had some brains. Which one was Sandstorm, and which was Gambit? Also, dumbest names ever.

Frankie begrudgingly gave her keyboard a few strokes. "I've got the camera looping now. You won't be seen."

"Alright, we'll let you know when we're out of there."

And then silence. How like these boys. At least Foxy would keep her on the line, let her hear what was going on. Frankie would often mute herself once Fox had entered the ventilation shaft, so she didn't distract her. But those days were over. She rubbed at an ache in her chest, then boxed the feelings up and tucked them away. There was no point in dwelling on them.

She went back to her book, a thriller about a deadly virus. Before she knew it, Gambit and Sandstorm were back in her ear.

"We're done, Eraser."

"Let me know when you're on the other side of the building. I don't want the cameras to catch you leaving when I turn them loose."

"Oh, right. Hang on."

Frankie muted herself and slapped her forehead. Really, these guys were idiots.

"Okay, we're back in the car."

"Good." She released the cameras and let them start recording again. "Have a good night, fellas."

But those rude little boys had already hung up.

Frankie started logging out of the syndicate's systems for the night. Her payment would hit the anonymous account and then she could transfer it over like she always did. She never took payments in her real name. Their criminal organization kept a tight leash on members' knowledge of each other, using code names only.

Before she logged out of the server, she saw a file with an intriguing name. It had today's date. When she tried to open it, she got asked for a password. Strange. It took seconds to crack the password on the file with her generator. Opening it up, she saw an invoice. Whoa, that wasn't the amount of money they usually paid her. What would she have to do to get money like *that*?

Looking it over, she got confused by the items listed. They didn't seem to have any rhyme or reason, or a reasonable definition. What the hell?

Should she reach out to Larry and ask him? Nah, that would just get her yelled at for looking at something outside of her jobs. But now her curiosity was piqued. What the hell was the syndicate hiding from its own people?

DAYS LATER, SHE GOT the notification that Sly Fox had popped into her private communication channel.

Frankie logged in right away. "It's about time, bitch."

There was a beat of silence, as though Sly Fox needed a moment. "Is this line private, Eraser?"

Frankie scoffed. "Come on, you know me. It's encrypted to hell and back. I protect my information better than Fort Knox."

She heard a rush of air like Foxy had let out a breath. Meanwhile, Frankie's curiosity was killing her. The syndicate never offered anyone a chance to come back if they left. Mostly because no one left unless they were in a body bag.

"What did they offer you to come back?"

"Come back? What are you talking about?"

"Well, I assumed that's why you called me."

"I don't understand. The syndicate ransacked my apartment and blew up my roommate's car, and you think they want me *back*?"

Frankie hummed at her former accomplice. "Let's put it this way, you're not dead. Clearly, you accepted their offer."

She growled low in her throat, just like a real fox. "There's been no offer, Eraser. I was traveling with someone, and they kidnapped him. No one's contacted me unless you count using my roommate's favorite lipstick to write creepy notes on the bathroom mirror."

Okay, that was messed up. "What the fuck?"

"Yeah, exactly. Where did they take him?"

Frankie grew quiet, the wheels in her brain turning. Something didn't add up. "Why should I help you, Foxy? You turned against us."

"I didn't turn against anyone, Eraser! I just wanted out."

"They said you went to the Feds."

"I didn't go to the Feds." While Frankie kept her talking, she located an email between Larry and his nephew. It gave her the address of the safe house where he'd wanted the Fox taken. Man, that noob had messed up.

She pulled up the cameras inside the warehouse and whistled. The guy in the chair was built and rugged. And he was pissed. "Where did you pick up this hunk of man meat?"

"You wouldn't believe me if I told you."

"Come on. Help a sister out." Frankie hadn't had any action in ages.

"You'll have to help me find him first." She paused, drawing out the suspense. "He's got brothers."

"Mm, no dice, Foxy. If you're not back with us, I can't assist."

"Then at least tell me why, Eraser. Why would they kidnap my friend?"

Eraser clucked her tongue as she looked back over the emails in Larry's account. Her idiot boss didn't know how to keep her out. "Looks like boss-man Larry figured out who you were with. We were tracking his credit card, and the hotel charge pinpointed your location. Apparently, his nephew lives in the area and was tapped to pick you up after his bar shift." She had to laugh. "Did you really think we wouldn't find you?"

"That doesn't explain why Roger was the one taken."

A few more clicks of the mouse gave Eraser the answer. "Apparently that idiot just sent a photo without indicating who he wanted in it. It's you and Hottie McHotterson."

Foxy groaned. "Please, Eraser, I need to get him out. He's not involved with this."

She shrugged, not that her former cohort could see her. "He might be persuaded."

A scoff. "He's a good man. Much better than any of us. He'll never join."

Frankie dropped the teasing tone. "Then he's not going to survive, and you know it."

Foxy was silent for a moment, but when she spoke again, Frankie's gut clenched.

"Look, Eraser, I didn't want to do this. But I will turn state's evidence if they harm a single hair on that man."

She hissed like an alley cat backed into a corner. "You'd never get immunity after what you've done. And you'd be signing your death certificate." Was that even true? Frankie didn't know. But now she was terrified.

Sly Fox kept talking. "In fact, he has a good friend who works at the FBI that is looking for you specifically. They could tell it was *you* who hacked the security cameras he put up around my apartment. And if you don't help me get him out of there, all I have to do is get this earpiece to that buddy and you're *all* going down."

Frankie inhaled a sharp breath as her blood turned to ice. "You wouldn't dare."

Except she knew Foxy would. "I'm done with this organization, and I won't go back. But I won't turn it in if they let me and Roger go."

She mulled this over. Could she survive if Fox turned them in? Maybe...

"Tick-tock, Eraser."

"Fine! I'll do it. But you need to tell me why you wanted out." Frankie hesitated. "The money's good, ain't it?"

"I'm thirty-five, you know. I'm not built to do all this crawling around and stuff anymore. That bullet last year was a wake-up call. I wasn't ready to meet my end on the wrong side of the law." Frankie heard the familiar zip of Fox's bodysuit. "Plus, something wasn't right. Where did they get that money? What were they doing with those gems? My gut told me to get the fuck out, so I did."

Frankie's thoughts churned. What about those strange files she kept finding that disappeared almost as soon as they'd been saved?

"You still there?"

"Yeah, I... I know what you mean. I've come across some... weird files. Coded messages. I haven't been able to crack them yet." Frankie wasn't sure what made her say the next bit, but as soon as it came out of her mouth, she knew it to be true. "But yeah, my gut's been screaming 'Something's wrong' at me, too."

Fox went silent while Frankie got lost in thought. Larry had been wrong about Sly Fox going to the FBI. But if she didn't help her, then she actually *would*.

Fuck, she was between a rock and a hard place.

"I'm ready. Are we doing this?"

"Yeah. Yeah, I'll help you get your man out." She tsked. "This must be some grade-A dick for you to risk your life like this." She couldn't imagine putting her ass on the line for a man.

"Alright. Which direction am I going?"

Instead of giving her the address, Frankie acted as her GPS through the tracker in her earpiece. She guided her through a series of twists and turns into the industrial district for the small town Fox and her man had led them to. But there was a method to her mad directions.

"There's no camera on this side of the building. It's an access road that isn't in use anymore."

"Thank you for that assurance," Fox bit out. Frankie could hear her teeth grinding and the bumps of the SUV going over the access road she'd sent her on.

That couldn't be comfortable. A pang of guilt made her lips loosen. "I just wanted to explain why I took you this way. That's all, Foxy."

"Just be glad you're not riding along in person," she grunted.

Watching the dot on her screen get closer to the destination, Frankie knew it was time for her to pull over. "Alright, that brick warehouse coming up at twelve o'clock is the one you want. Don't park too close."

"Got it." Foxy went silent while she parked the vehicle.

Frankie heard it turn off, and then listened as she pulled branches from the woods over the vehicle. That knife in her chest that had showed up when she learned Fox had left twisted again. "You know, if you'd come to me, I could have helped you get out."

She must have taken her old acquaintance by surprise. "What?"

Frankie hummed. "I got skills, you know."

"The point was no one was supposed to know."

"I just mean, we've worked together for years. I thought we were friends, so when Larry said you turned on us, it... it hurt, you know? I might not have understood at the time, but I could have helped you disappear. Wiped your information from the records so it was like Fox never existed."

She heard Fox gulp. "I'm sorry. I didn't realize I could…"

Frankie furrowed her brows. "You didn't think you could trust me?"

A snort came over the line. "I saw too many people stabbed in the back." After a beat of silence, she continued. "I'm really sorry, 'Racer."

"Naw, it's okay. I get it. They don't even let us exchange names. They don't want us to trust each other."

Foxy's dot started moving on Frankie's screen. "Let's save the sappy stuff for later. What's my entry point?"

"See that door with the keypad?" Frankie had pulled up the specs and was ready to enter the code to disarm the door.

"Yeah."

"When the light turns green, that means I've disabled the security system."

"Alright."

But as her fingers hovered over the keyboard, there was one thing she had to know. "Just answer me one more thing first, Foxy. What's so special about this guy, huh? Why is he worth leaving the syndicate and risking your neck?"

It took her a moment to answer. "He's a good guy, Eraser. Better than I deserve."

Eraser chuckled. That was more like the Fox she'd worked with. "But you're a bad enough bitch to take him, anyway." She clapped her hands together. "Alright, Foxy, let's do this. One last run, for old time's sake."

"Eraser? Call me Jenna."

She couldn't help her giggle. "And you can call me Frankie."

Chapter 2

Samuel Ivers carefully organized the last of his reports into the file folder with their case number and slipped them into the correct place in his file cabinet. As a cybercrimes specialist, he found it ironic how obsessed with hard copies the FBI was. Despite the encrypting technology available, and the servers they owned, the FBI wanted hard copies of everything. Or at least his office did. He didn't know how the other offices around the country operated.

The idea of transferring to a different office floated through his mind again, but he squashed it. In a matter of minutes, he'd be on vacation. And he didn't want to think about work until he got to Baltimore and met up with Roger for the first time since they'd both left the Army.

Knocking on his door interrupted his end-of-day cleaning. He gave a silent sigh when he caught the silhouette at the glass. Lachlan, his boss.

"Come in."

The door opened and Lachlan threw a familiar folder down in front of Sam. The folder for the case he'd just finished up.

He hoped his annoyance didn't come through his voice. Sam didn't want to burn any bridges yet. "What can I do for you in the next ten minutes, Lachlan? I'm getting ready to head out."

"You're absolutely sure this hacker has no connection to the theft ring?"

Sam closed his eyes and took a deep breath. Then he picked up the folder that was cluttering his desk and held it out for Lachlan. "You were there when I gave my report. Nothing's changed in the last twenty minutes."

"Ivers, I can feel it in my gut that this hacker is deeply involved with them. He's on their payroll."

Sam didn't deal with instincts. Not in this job. And he wasn't sure why his boss was trying to make this something other than it was. "Judges don't care about a gut feeling, you know that. I'm not changing my report in the last ten minutes before my vacation." Finally, his boss took the folder back from Sam.

While Sam worked in the cybersecurity department at the FBI, the organized crime division had borrowed him — without asking him if he wanted to help, he reminded himself bitterly — and tasked him with hunting down a jewel thief. A jewel thief! That was *not* his job. But Lachlan had seen the argument coming and explained that the thief had a hacker who would get into the targets' security systems and either erase footage or loop it so that the cameras didn't record any visuals.

He'd seen the tapes himself. It was extremely disconcerting to watch a big-ass ruby or sapphire sitting in its case safe as you please in one frame, and then in the next frame, poof! It vanished. Whoever this hacker was, they were skilled. But not skilled enough to not leave a trail.

It hadn't been more than breadcrumbs. Sam had just about gone cross-eyed before he found it. Just the slightest code change created this hacker's signature. But once he saw it, he couldn't un-see it. And he started to see it everywhere that the thief, known as the Sly Fox, had hit.

But then the trail disappeared without a trace. Fox had dropped off the radar. The FBI sure hadn't caught him. The more likely scenario was that he crossed someone and got himself killed. No one left an organized crime group unless they were in a body bag.

Until Roger called him with a problem. His principal, Jenna, had been the victim of a break-in. Whoever had done it had hacked Roger's security cameras and looped the video. And when he sent the files to Sam, he'd found this hacker's signature once more.

No one in that meeting had been happy with him when he announced that the hacker was a mercenary and not affiliated with the group stealing from museums. And clearly, Lachlan wanted to argue. But it completed his assignment and gave him the chance to take some much-needed time off. He couldn't wait until this nightmare was a distant memory.

The fact that he'd had over a month of leave saved up should be enough of a red flag. Sam had to get out. His job had taken over his life, like a kidnapper forcing him to sit at a computer eight hours a day. All he wanted at this point was a breath of fresh air. This Sly Fox project had about driven him crazy.

"Look, if you want someone else on the case, be my guest." As far as Sam was concerned, Lachlan and the organized crime division had gotten what they asked for.

He quickly checked the locks on his desk and file cabinet drawers, pulling on each one while his supervisor watched.

Everything had to be locked up tight each night before he left for the day. He had a perfect record for the last two years and he wasn't about to mess it up now.

Throwing his jacket on and opening the door to his office, Sam gestured for Lachlan to exit ahead of him.

"Have a nice trip, Sam." Lachlan's voice dripped with barely disguised anger. Whether it was at his insistence on keeping with his original analysis, or with Sam leaving them for a month, Sam didn't know. Nor did he care.

As of 5:01, that was no longer his problem.

IN HER DARK LAS Vegas basement apartment, lit only by the glow of her monitors, Frankie's natural curls swished around her head as she cracked her neck and popped her knuckles. Foxy and her man were safe and sound, back home in Baltimore. At least they better be. The apartment Fox had been staying in wouldn't be secure now that the syndicate knew where it stood. But the Sly Fox was too smart to stay there anymore.

She'd worked for the syndicate even longer than Frankie, after all.

Speaking of Foxy's former employer, and Frankie's soon-to-be former employer, she dove back into her search. She was back to researching those weird folders that had come across her screen, manifests of shipments written in an unfamiliar code. Fox — *no, Jenna* — said she'd left because she was done with the criminal life. That something had felt off for a while.

Those words had resonated with Frankie. Especially when these odd password-protected files had come up in her work. Emails back and forth with sums in the hundreds of thousands. *This* was where the syndicate made their real money. Not ransomware like what she did. Or even hacking into security cameras to clear the way for the members on the ground who stole valuables to be resold. That had been Foxy until a few months ago. Now, with Frankie's help, they would both eliminate their presence from the syndicate's files for good.

"Shoulda called me in the first place, girl." Frankie murmured to herself. But then, she had to admit, she hadn't started feeling funny about work until Fox disappeared off-grid.

Jenna had given her a secure email address so they could stay in touch directly, without the syndicate acting as a middleman.

At least by getting Larry and his two goons arrested, Frankie felt like she'd made up for her part in Jenna's apartment getting ransacked. So she felt better about sending the camera footage from the warehouse to the police email that night. The best part was that she'd bought her friend the opportunity to get away.

Unfortunately, it was only a matter of time before the syndicate figured out what Frankie had done. And that meant she had to get out fast.

But first, she wanted to know what they were up to.

Frankie's password-hacking software had been working overtime these past few weeks, as had Frankie herself. But it had paid off. She'd found a whole hidden server in the syndicate's network. Not only was the server itself password-protected, but every goddamn folder had layers of encryption. The process took forever, and every second counted. Anxiousness consumed her, urging her to vanish, and with every moment of delay, her nerves heightened.

But her curiosity *had* to be sated.

When her computer finally broke through the last layer of security, the early morning sun had started to peek through a crack in her blackout curtains. Frankie stretched her arms over her head and rubbed her dry eyes. She needed to go to bed soon.

But as the photo files loaded, her eyes widened. The files being large, their previews took time to populate. The more that loaded, the more her stomach swooped. Her energy drink turned bitter on her tongue, causing her to gag so hard, she had to slap her ebony hand over her mouth to keep everything down. This was just... Unbelievable. Her eyes widened, absorbing the horrifying display before her. The whir of her cooling fans echoed in the room, blending with the shallow, hurried breaths escaping her quivering lips. Her chest constricted and her skin grew cold and clammy as the photos multiplied on her screen.

Photos of women.

Now the shipment manifests made sense. The code would tell the reader age, race, hair, and eye color. Even body type, which the pictures showed as underfed, in her opinion. Their eyes stared into the camera, some red from crying. The ones that pained her the most were the ones that looked dead inside. They'd given up.

Frankie puked into her trash can until she dry heaved. Tears stung the corners of her eyes. She wiped them away with a takeout napkin lying near her mouse pad and then spat into the can to clear her mouth. It had been hours since she'd eaten, so there wasn't much to come up, thank God. She ran into the bathroom and rinsed her mouth out with water. When she stood and faced the woman in the mirror, she no longer recognized herself.

How did she get here? The two-bit hacker that only stole what she needed to survive had gotten a windfall when the syndicate recruited her online. She hadn't needed to steal identities in years thanks to this job.

They'd contacted her through a direct message on a hacking forum on the dark web. Flattered her, offered her a minor job that she'd completed with ease, then convinced her to work only with them for a serious bump in pay.

A faint memory of her birth mother crossed her mind. One of the few times she'd been sober. She'd looked at Frankie, who had seen something on a television infomercial that promised to make their lives easier. Her birth mother gazed at her with a soft look and said, "Frankie baby, if it sounds too good to be true, it usually is."

The overdose killed her not long after.

She'd forgotten that until just now. That must have been what happened. The jobs the syndicate offered were still crimes, but Frankie made way more doing jobs for them than just working on her own. At the time, their offer had seemed like her due. One of her more religious caretakers had often said, "Pride goeth before a fall." She'd never understood that line until now. Pride had led her down this pathway and now she was in bed with the devil.

Frankie shuddered. Those eyes in the photos would haunt her nightmares from now until eternity. She had to do something. Leaving the syndicate wasn't enough anymore. She'd been passed around through the foster system enough to know what it was like not to have any say in your own life. How could she stand by and do nothing while they abused and sold those poor women?

Her employer had crossed the line. She wouldn't, *couldn't,* walk away from this. There had to be a way to stop it. She might have been involved with it, but no more. Frankie would bring the whole syndicate down if she had to.

She pressed a cool hand to her forehead. "Think, Frankie, think!" Who could she go to?

Jenna had twisted Frankie's arm into helping her by threatening to turn state's evidence, and the irony didn't escape her that Frankie was considering the same thing. But her boss had just bragged about members of the FBI coming on board — taking a bribe, in other words. If she turned the evidence into the wrong person, it could get swept under the rug; worse, she didn't have any information on the whereabouts of the victims. All she had were photographs and weird shipping lists. That wasn't exactly evidence.

Frankie knew what she had to do. She'd been working on a new RAT, one that was nearly undetectable. But just in case, she'd put in an extra back door, one that wasn't as well hidden. Once they found the decoy, they'd stop looking and her remote access would be secure. As much as she told Jenna she had no intention of going back into the syndicate servers, she'd need the option. This was so much bigger than she'd expected.

As the files transferred over to her external hard drive, Frankie stared into the eyes of hundreds, possibly thousands of women, and some young men. They were dirty, too skinny, with ropes and cuffs around their wrists. Mattresses on the floor reminded her too much of the crowded group home where she'd spent her teen years. Shivering at the memories that threatened to overwhelm her, she copied the invoices over, intending to comb through them later to figure out where they had sent the victims. Right now, she needed to plant her code and erase her tracks completely. Even Jenna's Fed friend wouldn't be able to tell she'd been there when she was through.

She pushed her energy drink to the side. She wouldn't sleep in this place again — if she ever slept at all after this revelation. Frankie was used to leaving places quickly. It helped that the apartment came furnished, and she'd always traveled light. Who needed a ton of clothes when all you did was work from the computer all day or night? She'd never settled anywhere for long. The fact she'd been with the syndicate as many years as she had was odd now that she thought about it.

The only thing she'd need to ship would be her three twenty-seven-inch monitors. She checked the time and realized Baltimore would be three hours ahead of her. Jenna *should* be up. She hoped.

Jenna answered on the first ring. "Hello?"

"Jenna, it's Frankie."

"Frankie! Hey, girl."

"Is that offer to visit still open?"

"Sure is. Everything okay?"

"Can I bring my monitors?"

"Uh, sure. You, uh, you have work to do while you're here? I'm not sure we're okay with that."

"No, I just don't trust my landlord." At least *that* was the truth.

"Sure, let me give you the address. When did you want to come?"

"Baltimore is a four-day ride from where I am, so give me at least that long?"

"Okay. I'll try to remember to let Roger know. His friend is supposed to come over now that the election is done. But there's plenty of room."

Frankie wasn't really listening except for when Jenna recited the address. "I'll be done with our old boss by the time I get done here."

Jenna immediately picked up what Frankie had laid down. "Great. I'll see you soon. Be safe."

"You, too." She smiled for the first time that morning since finding the files.

By lunchtime, the files had copied over, and Frankie had her escape plan in place. Both hers and Jenna's information had all disappeared — like they had never even worked there.

But she wasn't the only hacker the syndicate employed, and she knew how she'd hunt for one that had disappeared. So she spent the next few hours systematically wiping her digital footprint so that even her bank account wouldn't be traceable.

Frankie packed up her life into her backpack and her saddlebags; all the important things like her laptop, hard drive, and two-piece ergonomic keyboard with the rainbow lights. She used some of her clothes and towels to pad the monitors in a shipping box and then cleaned up her studio apartment. Her stomach growled, but as always, Frankie didn't have much food in the apartment. She never did learn how to cook. Once she got to the U-ship place, she'd grab food and find a hotel.

At least she didn't have to carry her stuff in garbage bags anymore.

Chapter 3

"Please return your tray to the upright position and fasten your seat belts. We will begin the descent to Baltimore-Washington International Airport momentarily." Sam woke from his nap when the announcement came over the loudspeaker. He rubbed at the crick in his neck from sleeping in the airline seat and gazed down at the world below.

A month of vacation. It finally hit him that he wouldn't have to go to the office for thirty days. Well, it wasn't really a vacation. It was more like a trial run of working for Hunt Security, which was owned by his Army buddy, Roger Hunt. Roger had been pestering him for a while to visit and to consider working for him. Apparently, he'd been turning down cybersecurity jobs left and right, not having the skills to do it himself. It sounded like easy money, and a better work/life balance than Sam had working for the FBI. Plus, having his old friend back in his life sounded like exactly what he needed.

Baltimore came into view, a riot of colors with the green-blue of the Chesapeake Bay in the distance. He needed this. The Rockies were pretty, and he'd always consider Denver his hometown, but the change of scenery would do him good.

Perhaps he *would* move to Baltimore.

God knew he didn't have a reason to stay in Colorado anymore. His mom had left Denver almost a year ago, splitting a condo in the Florida sunshine with her sister. Dad had been the one who kept her there, a hardcore Denverite despite his constant complaints about shoveling snow. They'd been in love and showed it in their own way. And since they spent a lot of his youth separated by his father's deployments, they had deserved to spend as much time together as possible. But Dad had been gone a few years now, and Sam knew she'd missed his Aunt June.

At least we'll be in the same time zone for a while. He needed to fly down and see her soon, too. And Aunt June was keeping them busy with the retirement community down there. He'd video-chatted with Mom just last night about their golfing trip.

When she'd asked him what he was up to besides work, the answer had surprised her for once. Blue eyes that matched his had lit up when he told her about the trip, and she'd promptly told him she wouldn't bother him while he was on vacation.

"You're not a bother, Mom," was his response. But she'd asked all kinds of questions, and he'd been grateful for the time difference since he had to get up super early to get to the airport in time for his nonstop flight.

Their conversation highlighted his need to find people he could see outside of work. But he didn't have many hobbies, and he didn't make friends easily. He was a quiet and introverted individual, often finding solace in solitary activities, such as reading or playing video games. His interests were niche and didn't align with those of his peers, making it difficult for him to connect with others on a deeper level. Despite his best efforts over the years, social interactions remained challenging for him, leaving him feeling isolated. Plus, he had a bad habit of putting his foot in his mouth often.

As the plane taxied to the gate, he sent a text to Roger to let him know he'd landed. He couldn't help but feel a sense of contentment at the idea of hanging out with his friend again. Even if it wouldn't be like the old days. Not that Sam would complain. He was too old to pick up women in bars like they had when they'd been active Army. And to be honest, he didn't have the luck of the rest of their unit. He'd been the least muscular and the most awkward at talking to women.

The hot redhead he'd just met in the bar downstairs rolled over onto one elbow.

"So, what do you do when you're not doing Army stuff?"

Jesus, pillow talk already? Sam hadn't even gotten the condom off yet. "Computer games. I read."

She wrinkled her freckled nose. "Computers?"

He shrugged and got up to throw the condom away. "Yeah, that's what I do for the military, too."

By the time he got back to the bed, she was already pulling her dress over her head.

"Where are you going?"

"I have a meeting in the morning, so I'm going home." She patted his chest. "I had a good time, soldier. See you around."

When he went back to that bar two weeks later, she was in there with her blonde friend again, chatting up a table of Marines. He swore that was the last time he slept with a uniform chaser. They always wanted the hero that charged in guns blazing, not the tech guy that worked behind the scenes. He'd never compare to his brothers-in-arms.

His parents had had a one-in-a-million love he was un-likely to find, and he was okay with that.

Since Roger and Jenna were together now, he didn't think a bar crawl was on the list of activities. What a relief. Speaking of the happy couple, he spied them standing by the baggage claim. He hadn't realized how short Jenna was. She was almost a foot shorter than Roger. And tiny. He shook his head. From what Roger had told him, Jenna had a mouth on her and she'd sassed Roger into falling for her. Sam wasn't sure how that worked, but it wasn't his business.

Roger clapped him on the back with a grin. "Good to see you, man."

"You, too."

Roger gestured at his girl. "You've met Jenna."

"Nice to meet you in person." He shook the short red-head's hand. Funny, he thought she'd had black hair when they chatted online.

She must have noticed his confusion. "Nice to meet you, too, Sam. This is my actual hair color. I dyed it when we were having those… issues."

"Smart." He gave a nod of approval. "I think I see my suitcase." He rushed over to the conveyor belt, grabbing the black Samsonite with the American flag tied on.

"You still have that thing?" Roger sounded amazed.

Sam just shrugged. "Hasn't fallen off yet."

Jenna cocked her head at Roger. "What are you talking about?"

"His mom made that flag and tied it on his suitcase one time he was home on leave. We all gave him shit for it when he got back to base."

"She knit it?"

"Crocheted." Mom could be a bit sensitive when people got her craft wrong.

Jenna patted his arm despite Roger's scowl. "They were just jealous."

Sam chuckled. He liked her already.

Roger led them out to the short-term parking lot for the airport, and Sam threw his bags into the back of the truck. "Extended cab, nice."

"Thanks," Roger replied. "I had to replace the one I got when we first signed on. I figured it was time for a grown man's truck."

Sam opened the back door and let himself into the truck. "Did your brother give you shit about buying another Chevy?"

"Only as much as I give him about buying a Ford." Roger grinned as he helped Jenna up into the front seat, then he jogged around to the driver's side and slid in himself.

"You hungry? We can stop for lunch somewhere."

"I could eat. Those pretzels on the plane aren't exactly filling."

"What are you in the mood for?"

"I'm not picky." Sam wasn't sure how to turn off his inner workaholic, and this highlighted how bad it had become. It had been so long since Sam hung out with anyone outside work besides his mother that he couldn't even think of where he wanted to go to eat. God, he had better make himself useful to Roger, so this worked out.

No wonder his mother was so worried.

"There's a burger joint on the way home. Sound good?"

"Sounds perfect."

Roger drove them to a little place in a strip mall that advertised build-your-own-burgers and gourmet sundaes. The hostess seated the three of them at a booth next to a window. Roger and Jenna sat on one side, and Sam took the other all to himself.

"How's this work?"

Roger pointed at the condiment stand with little pencils and order pads at the end of the table. "You just check off what you want and then put your name on it and give it to the server when you order."

Jenna passed out pencils and order sheets while Roger spoke, and Sam's eyes bugged out at the choices. "What's in these seasoning choices?"

"You can ask the server. I always get Angel Wings because it's just salt, pepper, and garlic," Jenna answered. She and Roger had their heads bent over their order forms, clearly having been here before.

"Okay." Sam looked over the bun and meat choices. Hey, he was in Maryland. Might as well see what the crab burger was about. A basic wheat roll sounded good, and gouda cheese wouldn't overpower the crab. He checked off the box next to iceberg lettuce, then moved onto the premium toppings. The caramelized onions tempted him, but then he saw grilled pineapple and something about that with the crab burger just sounded like heaven. And now, chips or the sweet potato fries? When the server came around for drinks, he had most of his form filled out.

"Hi folks, what can I get you to drink?"

Roger ordered water, Jenna requested a diet Coke, and Sam ordered a Sprite.

"Did you have any questions about the menu?"

Sam decided to keep it simple. "What seasoning goes best with the crab burger?"

"Oh, you have to get the Baywatch seasoning." The server giggled. "It's really just Old Bay." She was cute, but she was too young for Sam.

He checked off the Baywatch seasoning. "When in Rome," he said, looking at Roger, who smirked.

"Are you ready to put in your orders?"

The three of them looked at each other and nodded. Roger spoke for the table. "Yep." They passed their papers over to her, and she scanned them quickly, probably just making sure that they had their names written down.

"Okay, I'll put these in and be right back with your drinks." She gave them another smile and strode away.

"So, besides the obvious, what's new with you?" Sam asked his oldest friend.

Roger threw his arm around Jenna and grinned. "Nadia's boyfriend asked me to help him pop the question. We've got a whole LARP event planned to set him up for it. It's going to be epic."

"Aren't you a little old for that shit?" Sam had to laugh. When Roger had confided in him years ago about joining a live-action role play group, he'd thought he was nuts. But Roger had told him stories over the years about various events and it seemed he was still having fun.

"It's a good incentive to work out," Roger said and shrugged. "There are guys older than me at Armageddon."

Sam just shrugged. "Are your brothers going to be there for it?"

Roger's mouth tightened into a line. "Just Jonathon. Finn's deployed."

"I'm sorry." Roger had two younger brothers and a sister: Jonathon, Finn, and Nadia. While Nadia had been the only one to go to college, Jon and Finn had followed in Roger's footsteps and joined other branches of the military. "Finn is the Marine, right?"

Roger nodded. "I'm not worried. Mom didn't take the news well, though. He's stationed in Okinawa this year, so we haven't seen him much."

"That's rough," Sam said as their drinks appeared on the table. "How's your mom holding up?"

"I'm not sure. It hasn't been that long since we put him on the plane."

"How about you, Jenna?" Sam asked his friend's girl. He wanted to get to know her as well on this trip.

"My friend Frankie's coming to visit."

"When did she tell you that?" Roger's head snapped to look at her.

"Last night." Jenna grimaced. "She wasn't sure of the date yet, but I told her we have the space."

"No worries, little Amazon. I just wish you'd said something."

"You were in the shower when she called, and I just forgot." A delicate blush stole over her cheeks, and Sam had an idea that he knew exactly *why* she'd forgotten to mention it until now.

"Where is she a friend from?"

Jenna fidgeted in her chair. "She's a... former colleague. We worked together on a lot of projects, and we just clicked."

Sam nodded, wishing he had a work friend like that. But he had Roger, and soon he and Roger would be working together.

The server reappeared with a tray full of plates. "Here you go!" Sam's mouth watered as he took in his creation. He didn't hesitate to take a big bite. The flavors exploded on his tongue, and he groaned low in his throat.

Jenna chuckled, and Roger smirked. "Good, huh? What did you order?"

Sam looked over his burger at his friends. "Crab with pineapple. How about you?"

Roger hefted a bun dripping in sauce. "I got the bison with barbecue sauce."

"Grilled chicken." Jenna lifted a chicken sandwich to her mouth.

Sam shook his head and chewed another bite, slowly, to savor it. "This is awesome."

"Save room for a sundae," Jenna told him. "They're amazing."

He looked down at his plate, then back at her. "I make no promises."

Damn, they could convince him to move here on the food alone. The company and the new job prospect made it even more tempting.

Chapter 4

FRANKIE LOOKED DOWN AT the address she'd written down on paper, old-school style. Then she squinted at the street sign. This was their street, alright. She put her boot back up on the foot peg of her motorcycle and turned slowly down the gravel driveway.

Finally, *finally*, she could see the house that satellite imaging hadn't been able to get close to. Clearly, the man valued his privacy. Frankie respected that. But he'd issued the invitation for her to visit. It had taken her weeks, but she finally had the information she needed and erased herself from the syndicate.

Her findings had horrified her, and she knew Foxy would want to know about them. If Fox was the kind of woman Frankie thought she was, then she'd want to take the syndicate down, too.

This wasn't just a friends' catching up trip. She'd come here to find allies in her upcoming war.

Vehicles lined the front lawn and the gravel in front of the detached three-car garage. The unmistakable scent of meat cooking over a flame tantalized her nostrils. Well, shit. She hadn't expected to be crashing a party as well.

Sauntering around the house, she narrowed her eyes and tilted her head to the side. There on the back lawn was a group of grown men and women fighting each other in medieval armor and weapons. On her second look, the weapons appeared to be made of foam. Looking around, she recognized Roger from the photo on his website for Hunt Security. He manned the grill on the back patio, laughing with a redhead and pointing at the spectacle. Could they know these weirdoes?

They'd never exchanged pictures. She hoped it wouldn't take Jenna long to figure out who she was.

"Hey, foxy lady!" She called out with a grin. The redhead and Roger both turned to look at her.

"Frankie! You're here!" Yup, that was Jenna. She vaulted over the railing and ran to Frankie for a hug. "Perfect timing. We're just about to cook the burgers."

A lovely offer, but Frankie was there on business. "Listen, girlfriend, we gotta have a chat."

Jenna released her, her face sober. "About what?"

"Work," she sighed, looking at the crowd gathered. "But it can wait until after the party."

"Sounds serious."

Frankie just shrugged. "I didn't mean to crash. I should have called ahead."

Jenna waved her off. "There's plenty of food. Come on, I'll introduce you."

The party went well into the evening. Clean-up didn't start until the sun went down, but with all the people crammed around the table, it didn't take long. Then everyone was saying their goodbyes. Frankie hung back, trying to ignore the guilt creeping up at crashing the party. She'd long ago learned to ignore the discomfort at being the only Black person in a room. The Nevada foster system hadn't really cared about race when placing her, so she'd been raised by different races. These people all seemed cool. But then she brought up the faces of the women she'd seen on the camera and reminded herself her mission was more important than her comfort or pride.

After the party, the only people who remained at the house were Roger, Jenna, Frankie, and Roger's friend, Sam. Apparently, he was on vacation and staying in the house. As the guys drank beer and shot the shit in the living room, Frankie pulled Jenna aside and into the kitchen.

"You remember how I was going to investigate our... former employer?"

She nodded.

"Well, I found out what those gems were funding."

Jenna's brow furrowed. "What?"

Frankie leaned in, not wanting the guys to overhear them. "Trafficking."

Wide blue eyes met hers when she pulled back. "Do you have proof?"

She nodded. "I can't just drop it off with the authorities, though. They have people in their pocket and it's going to take time to figure out who'd be safe." Frankie had spent way too long trying to break all those passwords to just give it to someone who would sweep it under the rug.

Jenna's face had gone ghost white. It looked like the realization had taken a moment to fully hit her. "Oh, my God... sex trafficking?"

Frankie nodded slowly. "That's why I had to leave. I couldn't be a part of it anymore." A shudder ran down her back, and she had to force the images she'd seen away to ensure her delicious dinner didn't make a reappearance.

Jenna clutched her stomach like she might throw up. "What do we do?"

Frankie crossed her arms over her ample chest. "I'm going to end it. Are you with me?"

"Hell yes." Jenna reached out, and they clasped hands.

"Hell yes to what?" Roger asked as he and his friend wandered into the kitchen.

Frankie eyed the men. Jenna had vouched for Roger being a good guy, and he knew all about their past. Sam, on the other hand, was a stranger, and she didn't know how much he knew.

Jenna turned to her man. If she trusted Sam enough for him to be in the room, Frankie would trust her judgment. She'd second guessed Jenna once before and it had backfired pretty spectacularly.

"Frankie says the syndicate is running a human trafficking ring. She wants me to help end it."

The men's eyes about popped out of their skulls. "Count me in." Roger extended a sun-tanned hand the size of a dinner plate at her, and Frankie almost squeaked. As a short, plus-sized girl, she got intimidated by big men. That was why she was more comfortable behind the keyboard. But Roger's handshake was firm yet gentle, demonstrating a level of respect she wasn't sure she deserved.

"I'm in, too." Sam drew her attention his way. She'd been trying to avoid looking at that tall drink of milk all day. His blonde curls looked soft as hell, and he had serious blue eyes behind those wire frames. She briefly wondered what it would be like to climb that tree.

"And what do you do?" That came out wrong. She didn't mean to sound like a bitch. "I mean, I know what he does," she gestured to Roger. "But what about you?"

She swore his eyes twinkled. "FBI, Cybercrimes division. I'm visiting from Colorado."

Oh, good goddamn. Of course, she had to be attracted to a Fed.

Hang on a minute. Jenna had said Roger had a contact at the FBI when she threatened to turn state's evidence. Could this be the guy who caught her trail?

Frankie wondered if she'd gone from the frying pan right into the flame, but those women deserved all the help Frankie could give them.

She swallowed her pride and shook his hand as well, ignoring how well they fit together. "I'm sure I can find something for you to do. Like make this all legit, for instance."

Sam grinned, and the impact was devastating. She could feel her core clenching. "This sounds like fun."

"Not much of a vacation for you." Roger watched his friend.

"Are you kidding?" Sam stood back up from where he leaned on the island. Frankie watched his Adam's apple bob as he took a swig of his beer. "I have to go through too much red tape to get anything done at work. This sounds more like the good old days."

Frankie tilted her head to one side and looked back and forth between the guys. Jenna clued her in. "Roger and Sam were in the Army together. Special Forces."

Fuck, images of that white boy in a uniform were going in her spank bank. Tonight.

Speaking of which... "Hey, can you guys recommend a hotel near here?"

"Hotel?" Roger shook his head. "I have a perfectly good guest room that's still open."

"Oh, I couldn't..."

"No, I insist. This sounds complicated, and I know from experience that staying close to each other is good for these sorts of operations."

Jenna nodded. "Where's your computer? Let's get you set up."

Frankie pointed at the backpack she'd left in the house when they invited her to stay for dinner. Her laptop was one thing she never let out of her sight when she traveled.

Jenna turned to Roger. "You get her the Wi-Fi password, I'll get the air mattress."

Sam set his beer down with a sharp thwack. "Give her my room. I'll take the air mattress."

Frankie shook her head. "I can't kick you out of your bed." She wouldn't kick him out of any bed even if he snored and ate beans for dinner. "The air mattress is fine."

She'd slept on way worse when the going got tough. When she aged out of the system, all her money had gone into finding a place to live. The only thing she'd had to hack with was the cheap second-hand laptop her social worker had given her as a "graduation" gift. Their offices had been upgrading, and Miss Lisa had snagged a few decommissioned ones for her kids. A sleeping bag on the floor had been her bed for months until she got lucky on a dumpster dive.

Jenna rolled her eyes. "Don't go all stoic and macho on us, Sam."

He crossed his arms over his chest, unknowingly making his biceps flex. Smaller than Roger's, but nice all the same. "It's not right."

"And they say chivalry is dead." Frankie snorted. "I'm not making you move, dude. They didn't even know I was coming."

When he glowered (hell, even that was hot) and opened his mouth, Fox interrupted with a distraction. "Why don't we set up the computers in the same room? Like a command central."

Frankie could have kissed Jenna for the suggestion. At least she'd get some nice scenery while she worked, even though Sam was officially off-limits. No way could she bang a Fed. "Sounds good. Maybe you can learn a few things."

Sam lifted one eyebrow and stared down at her. "We'll see."

Frankie pulled up the shipment notification on her phone. "My monitors won't get here until tomorrow. But I can show you what I've got." She shuddered. "But it might be easier if you didn't see all of it."

"We need to know what we're up against." Roger leveled an intense look at her. "Or we can't help you."

Frankie bit her lip. "Alright. But not tonight." If she showed them her findings this late at night, no one would sleep. And after nearly four days of riding, she felt exhausted.

Jenna patted her on the shoulder. "Let's get you set up first, then. We're not going anywhere. It can wait until morning."

Frankie bid the boys good night, grabbed her backpack, and followed Jenna up the wide wooden staircase. Briefly, she wondered why a single guy would buy a family home. But it wasn't any of her business.

Jenna grabbed a box from the hall closet and opened the door to what looked like a storage room. Old boxes with labels like "Roger — first grade" sat stacked in the corner.

"I'll make Roger move his shit to the basement tomorrow. He should have cleaned these out ages ago." Jenna shook her head as she opened the box and removed an air mattress. Plugging the pump into the wall, it started to inflate.

Jenna turned around and went back into the hall. "I'll get you some sheets and a blanket. Did you want to shower?"

"That'd be great." Frankie tucked her pack next to an old chest of drawers. Were they Roger's from childhood? It had certainly seen its share of combat.

Her friend returned with a set of towels. "Knock yourself out. You've got a door to the bathroom right here." She opened a door Frankie hadn't noticed and walked inside.

"Ooh, fancy." Frankie immediately dug into her bag for her moisturizer and curl cream. Four days on the road had been hell on her hair.

Jenna rolled her eyes. "It's not really. You have to share with Sam in the other guest room." She gestured at another door on the opposite wall. "You can lock the door so he knows not to come in."

"Why would I do that?"

That made Jenna laugh. "I thought I sensed some tension there."

Frankie waved her off. "Don't worry, I'm not going to do anything about it."

"Why not?"

She dropped her voice to a low hiss. "He's a Fed!" When Jenna just blinked her eyes at her, Frankie smacked her palm against her forehead. "I ain't tryin' to go to jail, Foxy!"

Jenna's face scrunched up as she considered that. "Good point. I figured out Sam was looking for me when he told us he was following your trail."

Frankie bit her lip. "Does he know?"

Jenna shook her head. "I know he's Roger's friend, but ... I don't know if I can trust him that far yet."

"Roger doesn't care?"

"He says it's my business. And that Sam has a lot of integrity, so there is a chance he could turn me in." She shrugged.

Well, Roger just earned several brownie points with Frankie. Few men, in her limited experience, would choose their girlfriends over their friends.

"I'll let you get on with it. And I'll get your bed made up while you're in here."

"I can make it, babes." But Jenna just crossed her arms over her chest.

"Nope. You're a guest. Deal with it."

Frankie laughed, then locked the doors on both sides of the bathroom. She couldn't wait to scrub the road grime off.

Chapter 5

SAM WAITED FOR THE sink to turn off before he knocked on the bathroom door the following morning.

"Almost done!" That melodic voice, still husky from sleep, made Sam clench his fists and lean his forehead against the doorjamb. It might have been the engagement party the night before, but he'd traced those curves dozens of times with his eyes, wishing he could use his hands instead. She carried herself like she had secrets, at least when she thought no one was watching. And Sam liked nothing more than cracking a puzzle. That's why the technological side of war had drawn him twenty years ago.

That she had a body like a back road and thick plump lips was just the icing on the cake, as far as he was concerned.

"All done!" came the call as the door lock clicked open. Sam shook his head and waited a beat for her to leave the bathroom so she wouldn't see his morning wood. His thoughts hadn't helped the situation.

He brushed his teeth and washed up in a hurry, then debated his clothing options. He opted for practicality over comfort; his jeans would do a much better job of reining in his dick if he got distracted during this discussion.

Following the smell of coffee and bacon, he descended the stairs and swung into the kitchen, the last to arrive. Roger stood at the stove, scrambling eggs while a pile of crispy goodness dried on paper towels next to him. Jenna and Frankie sat at the kitchen island, steaming mugs in their hands.

"Morning, ladies. Roger." Sam had only been there two days, but he already knew where the mugs were. He poured himself a cup and leaned back against the counter.

"Breakfast is almost done."

Sam turned back around and pulled plates down from the cabinet before Jenna could get out of her seat.

"I can get them, Sam."

"But I'm right here." He smirked as he laid them down next to the stovetop. "And I don't need the step stool to get them."

He turned just as Jenna stuck her lip out and glared at him. "Rude."

Sam chuckled. "I'm not a guest. I'm a brother, remember?"

Jenna just rolled her eyes. "That doesn't count."

"Just let him help, Princess." Roger shook his head as he plated the eggs and bacon. He slid a plate in front of the empty seat across from Frankie and gestured at Sam to sit.

Settling onto the bar stool, Sam had a front-row seat to Frankie's discomfort. She nibbled at the bacon and mostly pushed the eggs around on her plate. "What's wrong?"

Frankie glanced up at him, then back at her food. "I haven't had much of an appetite since I found these files."

Sam swallowed the desire to wrap her in his arms and tell her they were going to fix it. He was so out of line. What the hell was up with him? There was just something about her he couldn't put his finger on. She was reeling him in like a fish on the line. Deciding more coffee was the answer, Sam took a heavy pull from his mug.

"Why don't you tell us what happened?" Jenna asked.

Frankie took a deep breath. Her shirt with the words "My password is the last eight digits of Pi" stretched over her luscious breasts. Sam quickly averted his gaze to her face. But she wasn't looking at anyone while she spoke.

"Things started feeling … different once you left, Jenna." Jenna nodded, though Frankie focused on her breakfast. "Then I came across these strange files. Shipping manifests. Hundreds of thousands of dollars of product sold, but the item lists didn't make any sense." She opened her laptop, which Sam hadn't realized had been sitting next to her this whole time. A few clicks, and she turned the screen around to face them.

Sam squinted at the screen. The odd combination of letters and numbers didn't make sense to him, either. She turned the computer back around.

"So I went deep diving. It turned out they had hidden a server on the network. Only people who knew about it would know where to find it." Then she shrugged, one side of her mouth lifting in a sly smirk. "Except me." She fiddled with the laptop some more, huffing a deep breath while they all held theirs.

"It took days just to break the password. Especially since I still had to do jobs for them to make sure they didn't suspect anything was amiss. But that was just the beginning. Every file had layers of encryption, and it took ages to break through it all."

Sam chewed his food while he listened. Anyone with that much security definitely had something to hide. Not unlike the government.

"I didn't figure out what those manifests meant until I saw the pictures."

"Pictures?" Jenna looked even paler than normal. Sam looked at Roger, who met his gaze, his face a grim mirror of his own. Sam put down his fork and swallowed his food.

"Don't choke, girl." Frankie laid her hand atop Jenna's coffee cup. Then she turned the screen around.

"Oh, my..." Jenna gasped.

But Sam wasn't watching the two of them. While he glanced at the pictures — and they were absolutely horrifying, make no mistake — he was watching Frankie. Her deep brown eyes glittered with a ferocity he hadn't seen in a person since his Special Forces days.

"So I left, too. And I want to take them down."

Roger spoke next. "What do you need?"

Frankie shrugged and turned that intense gaze on Sam. "You tell me. Is this enough for a conviction?"

Sam scrubbed his hand over his face. He wasn't the right type of investigator, but he'd learned a few things from his time at the Bureau. "We need names of the players involved. A physical location would help, too." This was so much more important than the Sly Fox case. These weren't gems being stolen, they were living, breathing *people*. He started going through a mental Rolodex of people he knew he could trust. "You mentioned something last night about them recruiting agents?"

She nodded. "At least that's what Larry bragged about. Said they bribed a few agents to sweep anything to do with the organization under the rug." She shuddered. "I just can't... Can't let this go."

"I understand." This was the exact reason Sam had joined the cyber team at the FBI. Although the crimes they investigated tended to be more financial in nature, at the very least, they were less personal. "Pull up the manifests again, please?"

Frankie switched tabs, and Sam looked at the item lists again. The letter F or M, followed by a two-digit number, followed by another alphanumeric code that he realized worked out to a description of the person in question.

He gulped. Some of those victims were minors. Jesus Christ, what monsters. How the hell did nice women like Jenna and Frankie get mixed up with a group like *this*?

He'd have to ask Roger later.

"Let me make some calls," he said finally, his appetite gone. "I'll see who I can get to take the info as an anonymous tip and then we'll see what all we need to find."

"In the meantime," Roger added, "let's take the fourth bedroom and get the computers set up there."

Jenna looked at him sideways. "You only have one desk."

"I think I got a folding table in the garage somewhere. If not, we'll go buy one."

Frankie closed her laptop and nodded. "My monitors should be here by the end of the day."

Sam looked over at her. "I think our first order of business is to make a list of where they're shipping people from, and who they're being shipped to. You're probably the one with the best chance of decoding that."

Frankie nodded. "I got you."

"And eat." Sam pointed at her nearly full plate. "You need fuel to save them."

Frankie bit her plush bottom lip, and Sam shifted in his seat. "I'll try."

He just nodded and went upstairs to find his work phone. He'd debated bringing it at all, but now he was glad that he had.

Turning on the government-issued cell, he thumbed through his contact list until he got to the one he wanted. Ross had been part of his orientation when he first joined the FBI. They'd bonded over Army stories, but Ross worked in the field and Sam just worked behind a screen. They'd worked on the same case once or twice over the years. He answered on the first ring.

"Patterson."

"Hey, Ross, how's it going?"

"Sam! Good to hear from you. How's Denver?"

"I'm technically on vacation, visiting an old army buddy in Maryland."

"Get out! I just got a transfer and moved back to my old hometown there."

"That's great, Ross. Listen, I got a question for you."

"Shoot."

"A friend of my friend has reason to believe they've uncovered a human trafficking ring. But the organization in question apparently has some of our agents on their payroll. He's looking to me to get it to the right person who won't sweep it under the rug."

Ross let out a low whistle, and Sam could practically hear the gears turning over the line. "You know we can only investigate federal crimes, right?"

"I'm pretty sure this qualifies."

"Did they cross state lines with them?"

"Not sure yet. They wrote the shipping manifests in some kind of code. We're going to try to break them."

"If it's happening in my area, I'll take your info straight to my boss. He's solid. But we have to prove it's big enough."

"Thanks, Ross. I appreciate that. I'll get in touch once we know more."

"Sure. Let me give you my personal number."

Sam plugged the digits into his own personal cell and shot Ross a text. "There. Now you have mine as well."

"Good luck. And try to enjoy your vacation, huh?"

"I'll try..." His voice trailed off as he recalled the images of the women tied up. "There were photos, Ross. And I think some victims are minors... I just can't turn my back on this."

"I understand," Ross murmured. "Do what you have to."

"Always. Take care."

"See you around."

Ross hung up the phone, and Sam breathed a sigh of relief. If Patterson trusted his boss to be faithful, that was good enough for Sam. His own wouldn't be able to help, since this wasn't his division. But Ross's superior could.

Now he just needed the information for the bureaucrats.

Chapter 6

Frankie looked longingly over at the powerful CPU tower that Roger had set up for Sam. As fast as her Viviobook was, it was no Alienware. But portability was necessary when you moved around as much as she did. And sometimes she had to be within a certain range to hack a system.

Not that she'd ever tell Sam that.

Her monitors had come in late that afternoon, giving Roger enough time to dig out a long folding table from the garage and source a computer chair from... somewhere. Honestly, Frankie didn't give a shit.

It was clean; it was comfy, and that's all she really cared about.

By evening, she had her laptop set up just the way she liked it. The extra cooling fans sat under the laptop. Her three monitors gave her plenty of space to work, her glowing keyboard and matching mouse having a rave under her hands. A bag of Doritos lay to her right and her energy drink sat on her left.

Frankie cracked her knuckles. "Alright. Time to work."

Then the overhead light clicked on.

Her head snapped to the side, where Sam stood next to the door. "You're welcome."

She pursed her lips in agitation. "Thanks. Can you turn it back off?"

"But you're working."

"Yeah. And the darkness helps me focus."

He crossed his arms and leaned against the doorway. "If by focus, you mean destroy your eyesight."

"No, I don't. Now if you want these manifests figured out..." She let her voice trail off and gestured at the switch. He was a smart boy. He could pick up what she was putting down.

"Well, I have to work, too, and I can't stand a dark room with a bright screen. It gives me headaches."

"Ugh, if you say so." She waved him off. "Have it your way."

He walked around to Roger's desk and sat down. "Your eyes will thank me later."

For now, they rolled in her head as she settled back in her chair and tried to think.

What the hell could that gibberish on her screen mean? Were the numbers coordinates, or some back-ass-ward way of obscuring an address? And it had to be the address because of the placement on the invoice.

Sam's computer made a noise, and then the typing started. Frankie was so used to being the only person in the room that she hadn't realized how sensitive her focus was. Shaking her head, she dug around in her backpack and pulled out her noise-canceling headphones.

She started searching for the numbers just by going to Google. Surely something would come up and give her a clue.

Two hours later, Frankie slumped in her chair, holding her head in one hand while she stared at her computer vacantly in disbelief. Nothing. She was no closer to figuring out where they were shipping people from than she was at the beginning. Her brain felt like mush. She sighed and rubbed her hands over her face.

Frustration bubbled up in her chest. She spent years of her life in front of the screen, breaking into security systems and servers, but for some reason this stupid encrypted address had her stumped. Frankie might as well be a fish trying to climb a tree.

She rubbed her forehead and pulled her headphones off as a headache started to bloom.

"You all right?"

"This is ridiculous. I don't think this gibberish even means anything."

She reached for her beverage, but it wasn't there. Looking up, she saw Sam holding it while he stood at the side of her makeshift desk. "What the hell?"

"First, too much caffeine has been known to cause headaches. Second, it was way too close for comfort to your laptop. I watched you nearly spill it six times."

"It was fine!" she blurted out through clenched teeth. "Mind ya business." She'd never lost a laptop to a beverage. Mainly because drinks never lasted long around her.

"Maybe you should join me in the kitchen for some water."

"Maybe my foot should join your head up your ass!"

He actually stepped back at that. Good. Frankie was in no mood to play.

"That's not yours. Give it back."

Sighing, he handed over her can with a roll of his eyes. "What's giving you trouble?"

She took a loud sip and gestured at the screen as if she had already told him. Which she had. "I can't figure out what these codes mean."

"You don't have a cipher?"

"A what?"

"It's how you code and decode messages like this. I thought since you used to be affiliated with the organization, you might have access to it."

"Never heard of it." Cipher. That's what the thugs in her old neighborhoods would call a five-dollar word.

"You didn't see anything on the server that looked like one?"

Frankie shook her head. "I wouldn't even know what to look for."

Sam strode back to his computer and waved her over. "I'll show you."

Reluctantly, she stood and wandered over behind his desk. On the screen was an image of letters and numbers.

"That's weird," she said. "Why is A labeled with a 3?"

"Because that's the code." Sam pushed his glasses up his nose and pointed at the screen. "Each letter corresponds to a different number. The sender encodes their message, with numbers, then sends it to the recipient. When the recipient goes to read it, the cipher tells them what the letters mean."

Frankie peered over his shoulder. "It's a key."

"Yes, that's another name for it." He sounded flustered.

"Well, then, why didn't you just *say* that?"

"Key is a generic term, especially where computers are involved. I wanted to be clear."

"Clear as mud, more like," she muttered. Louder, she said, "No, I don't have the key. No one there uses this kind of encryption normally. Besides, that doesn't explain the numbers and symbols in the original message."

Sam raised his hands. "I only pulled up a simple cipher in order to explain the concept. Clearly, what we're working with is far more sophisticated."

Frankie rolled her eyes again where he couldn't see. So far, *she* was the only one working on it. But she didn't bother pointing that out.

Actually, maybe she should put him to work.

"Then what do you suggest?"

He threaded his fingers through his curls, tugging on them a bit. "I would start by hunting for the cipher in their servers." He pursed his lips. "Do you still have access?"

Frankie nodded and sighed. "I don't like going in there. Especially now that I've left."

"I understand that. But I don't know if we have another option. Unless we can find another way to break the code, which I doubt, we won't be able to figure out where they're operating from."

"It changes anyway." Frankie reminded him. "The address is different depending on which invoice you're looking at."

"Once we break the code, we can decode all of them. That's the proof my colleague will need to take to his boss."

"Really?"

"Yes. The FBI won't get involved unless we can prove they're transporting their victims across state lines."

"What about if they take them out of the country?"

Sam's eyes widened, and he huffed out a breath. "Then we'll probably have to reach out to each country's law enforcement as well. Maybe Interpol."

"Damn." That was a lot of red tape. Frankie hoped to stay the fuck away from all of that. Drop the information and then disappear again.

And to do that, she had to get back into the server. But which one? She mulled it over as she pulled up the software she jokingly referred to as her "cloaking device" — a virtual private network that scrambled her IP address every five minutes, or however often she told it to. Anonymity was essential here.

Her first instinct said they wouldn't keep the cipher on the hidden server, but wouldn't someone question it if they came across it in another one? Why give anyone a reason to look for it? Either way, there were plenty of places to look. She'd start with the hidden server and do a file search, but didn't expect that to yield any results. Chances were, no one was dumb enough to actually save the file with cipher, key, or code in the name. Then she'd comb through looking for any files that seemed out of place.

Frankie slid her headphones back on over her ears. Time to get back to work.

SAM TOOK HIS GLASSES off and pinched the bridge of his nose. This, *this* was why he was single. Every time he opened his mouth around an attractive woman, he managed to fuck it up.

How had Frankie, whom Jenna had described as the IT genius of their former employer, not understood what a cipher was? It was rudimentary code vocabulary. Fuck, he'd had one of those silly decoder rings from some cereal company when he was a kid. He'd had great fun sending coded messages back and forth with... his mom.

He hadn't had a lot of friends growing up. Hell, he didn't have a lot of friends now. The only child of older parents, who had given up on having children years before he came along, he'd had trouble relating to kids his own age. The Army had helped, but the only real friend to still talk to him from those days was Roger. The rest had disappeared into their lives, never to be heard from again now that they weren't part of the same unit.

So what if he had preferred a good book to a sports match on television? Roger had made an effort, noticing the book Sam was reading and talking to him about it. They had the same taste in authors and would discuss various books over beers while the other guys in their unit lured skirts to the table. Sam was no virgin, but he had never had a relationship. Once the physical release of sex was complete, he didn't have much to talk to those girls about. And then they would be on to the next guy in uniform.

His people skills were lacking. Sam knew it. He'd already insulted Frankie once, and it was going to get worse. Because he needed order in his office space. Frankie had her stuff strewn about haphazardly. It drove him batty when people ate or drank around the computers. And that energy drink of hers, which was probably pure poison, had nearly taken a tumble for the seventh time now. Not to mention the crunching sound from her eating chips and the crumbs she must have stuck in her keyboard.

Perhaps it was a result of the rules at his office, and during his time in the Army. After years of not being allowed food or drink anywhere near the desk, he expected it to be a matter of common sense.

But as Dad had been fond of saying, common sense wasn't common anymore.

He fought to tune her out and focus back on the penetration test he had promised to do for Roger's client. While Frankie was focused on their humanitarian mission, he was still on a test run for Hunt Security.

Hours later, he called it a night. Frankie had left an hour earlier, at Jenna's behest. She'd wanted "girl time" and had lured Frankie downstairs with promises of margaritas and chips. Back in his room, he decided to grab a shower. He stripped and left his clothes in the pop-up hamper he'd brought with him. Grabbing a clean pair of boxer briefs, he slipped into the shared bathroom. Frankie's door was already shut, so he didn't think about it.

After laying the bathmat down, Sam stepped into the shower. Just as he was bending over to turn on the water, Frankie's door slammed open. She didn't even see him in the shower as she headed to the sink. But he couldn't look away.

She wasn't wearing a shirt.

Red lace outlined her generous tits, the leggings she wore hugging her equally plush ass.

He had zero control over his reaction. His cheeks grew hot, and his jaw dropped. The choking sound coming from his throat did not sound entirely human. It drew her eyes up from the shirt she was rinsing in the sink to the mirror, which meant she watched through the glass shower door as his cock sprang to attention.

She gaped at him for a moment while the water ran over her hands. Then she slapped one over her eyes. "I'm so sorry it wasn't locked. Why wasn't it locked?"

Gasping for air, she shut the water off and hastily squeezed the water out of her shirt. "Never mind, I'm going."

Then she bolted from the room like her ass was on fire, locking the door behind her as she went.

Sam groaned and smacked his head against the tile wall. He wanted her, but her reaction said everything. That wasn't going to happen. But this raging thing had a mind of its own. Sam considered his choices. One, he could relieve himself, but he knew it would be Frankie in his mind. Two, he could just hose down his little soldier. Sam shook his head and leaned back over, turning the water on cold to drive his erection down. The idea of jerking himself to the image of a woman who'd made it clear she didn't want him left a sour taste in his mouth.

After his cold shower, Sam propped himself up to read the latest fantasy novel by his favorite author before he fell asleep.

Chapter 7

"Hey, you two, come get some lunch!" Jenna's voice called up. Frankie almost said she wasn't hungry, but then her stomach growled. She pushed herself away from her desk and rose, her body stiff. After a day and a half of combing the entire hay field for the proverbial needle, Frankie was ready for a break. She broke the connection to the syndicate's servers and then followed Sam downstairs.

She hadn't been able to look him in the eye or speak to him all morning after the mortifying incident last night. It had been a complete accident. Her focus had been on the queso staining her shirt, which was why she forgot to knock before barging in on the man in the buff.

And damn, buff was the word. She'd had to check her chin for drool before returning downstairs with a fresh shirt. Then she proceeded to drown the images assaulting her mind in tequila.

No banging the Fed, Frankie.

In the kitchen, Jenna had laid plates and sandwich fixings out on the island and was making herself a ham on rye. Frankie thanked her and reached for the sourdough, only to bump her hand into Sam's as he grabbed it at the same time. "Sorry," they said in stereo.

Sam removed his hand and gestured for her to go first. "After you."

"Thanks." She quickly took two slices and handed him the bag, ignoring the warmth of his skin. Damn, this would be a lot easier if she could hate him. But he was the perfect gentleman outside of their office. And the walls had been starting to feel like they were closing in on her today.

Roger's house was gorgeous, but Frankie needed out. Eyeing the clear blue skies outside the window, she knew just what she needed.

"I'm going for a ride after lunch."

"That sounds like fun. Have you had any luck?" Jenna offered her the mayonnaise.

"No breakthroughs yet. I need to clear my head." She spread some of the mayo on one of her slices of bread, then piled turkey, cheese, and some lettuce on top. There.

"Gotcha." Jenna nodded as she offered it to Sam, who shook his head while he slathered mustard over his bread. "I can't imagine being cooped up all day like this and not going insane."

"You get used to it," was Frankie's response. When she was on a job, she didn't dare get distracted. So her focus was intense. But the fact was she hadn't left her old apartment between the night Roger got kidnapped and the day she said goodbye to Vegas for good. While the four-day trip had been nice, she hadn't thought once about the scenery. She'd just been trying to get to Jenna and Roger as fast as humanly possible.

No one could go balls to the wall forever.

As Frankie savored her food, she noticed Jenna grinning at her phone and typing to someone. "You talking to your man?" She asked with a smirk.

"Yup," Jenna answered and turned the phone face down on the counter.

Ooh, Frankie bet it was dirty. "What are you up to?"

"Nothing! He said he should be home in a couple of hours. They're almost finished."

Sam looked up from his sandwich. "Good, I need to talk to him about that test I ran for the client."

"I'll let him know you're done."

Sam waved her off. "I can tell him when he gets home. It's not urgent."

Jenna shrugged and went back to her lunch. Frankie polished hers off and got up to take her plate to the dishwasher.

"Frankie! I can do that!"

She had it in before Jenna could get out of her seat. "It's fine! I've been here two days after all. You don't need to wait on me."

Jenna leaned her chin on her hand and pursed her lips. "Until I get my license, I can't exactly go out on jobs with Roger. I'm bored."

Frankie snorted. "You'll have it soon, right?"

"It should come in the mail any day."

"Relax, girl. Now, I'm going for that ride. Then I'm coming back to look for that code key."

She refused to call it a cipher in front of Sam again. The twitch in his brow was totally worth it.

Laughing to herself, Frankie sashayed in her skinny jeans over to the front door, where she zipped up her boots and slid her leather jacket on over her t-shirt. She took her helmet off the hook on the wall, waved goodbye as she shut the door behind her, and headed for her bike where it sat next to the garage.

Snapping her helmet strap under her chin and zipping up her leather jacket, Frankie turned the key and kicked up the stand. She crept along the long-ass gravel driveway so that the rocks didn't fly up and hit her. Once she reached the pavement, she was off.

Frankie's stress melted away as the miles rolled by. She wandered from Roger's land covered in trees along the highway, then took an exit through various suburbs, making her way toward Baltimore proper. Out of curiosity, she even drove past the row house Jenna had been living in, where Frankie had hacked the cameras. Had it really only been a few weeks since then? Frankie shook her head at the lies the syndicate had told them to get people to turn on one of their own. Of course, the lie was that Jenna had turned on *them*.

Ugh, enough thinking about work. She pulled out in front of a bus and kept heading for the bay. Frankie wanted to see the water.

As a foster kid growing up in the desert, she'd been obsessed with the beach. But none of her foster families had the money or the inclination to take them on a vacation. The Chesapeake Bay wasn't the beach, but it was water, and it led to the ocean. It would do.

The sun shone in the sky as Frankie rode through what appeared to be the warehouse district. She stopped at a stop sign and stared up at huge black and rust-orange ships docked behind the warehouses. She'd never been this close to one. They could hold several city blocks on the deck alone. She wasn't sure how long she sat there in awe, but the beep of a horn behind her let her know she'd been there too long.

It was there along Nicholson that she heard the pop. Her bike swerved off to the side. Her heart racing, Frankie brought the bike under control and pulled to a stop along the sidewalk. She flipped her hazard lights on and put the kickstand down. When she stood on the sidewalk, she swore. Her tire must have hit some debris on the road. It hadn't just gone flat; it was shredded, leaving a trail of rubber about twenty feet down the street. She'd be lucky if she didn't need a whole new wheel.

Frankie pulled out her phone and checked the time. Roger had that big truck, and he should be back from that job by now. She opened the contact she'd added her first morning in town and hit the dial button. It rang and rang, and then she got his voicemail.

Hanging up, she tried Jenna's phone. What the hell? She got her voicemail, too! Dialing Roger again, she half-expected it to go to his message again, but someone picked up right on the last ring.

"Frankie? Everything okay?"

She groaned internally. "Sam, why are you answering Roger's phone?"

"Roger's... indisposed at the moment."

Great. "I got a flat tire, and I wanted to ask if he could come get me. My bike should fit in his truck easily."

"No problem." Keys jingled in her ear. "Let me write him a note and I'll be on the way."

She snorted. "Isn't borrowing without asking stealing?" There was no way he'd ever do such a thing.

Sam sighed. "Well, unless you'd like to wait for him and Jenna to come out of the bedroom, I don't see what choice I have." He paused and Frankie felt her cheeks get hot. "Look, you'd be doing me a favor by giving me an excuse to get out of the house. I really don't want to be here right now."

"Alright. I'm on Nicholson."

"Can you give me an address?"

She rattled off the cross street while he plugged her location into his phone.

"I'll be there as soon as I can."

"Great. Th-thank you, Sam." She swallowed past the lump in her throat.

"You're welcome."

They ended the call, and Frankie leaned against the telephone pole. Too bad there wasn't a café or something around here where she could wait comfortably.

She hooked her helmet over her arm and occupied herself by playing games on her phone. When a big silver pickup pulled up and parked next to her bike, she jumped, then relaxed when she saw Sam behind the wheel. He opened the door and came around to let the tailgate down, then pulled a plywood sheet from the bed.

"Hey, Sam. Thanks for the ride." She watched his muscles flex as he lifted the bulky sheet of wood.

"You're welcome. Let's get your bike loaded."

The plywood sheet had hooks in the end so it wouldn't slip off the tailgate, creating a makeshift ramp. She'd have to ask Roger about why he had that sitting there.

Frankie put the bike in neutral so they could wheel it around and up the ramp, hoping like hell it would hold the weight. The board shivered and shook when she walked the bike up into the bed of the truck, but it held. Then Sam unhooked it and jumped into the bed with her, laying the sheet down while she lashed the bike in place with the bungee cords he handed her.

When everything was situated, Frankie turned to face him for the first time since the shower incident. "Thanks again. I didn't know who to call for a tow."

Sam nodded. "You're welcome. And we'll ask Roger when we get back. I seem to recall his future brother-in-law works on motorcycles. He'll know who to call for a new tire." He jumped back down to the ground, then held his hand out to her.

"I'm good." Frankie didn't want to take his hand for anything. Things were awkward enough. She turned her back and lowered one leg down to the pavement.

But the pavement was a lot further away than she'd realized. Her foot groped through the air, reaching lower and lower, until she lost her grip on the side of the truck! She fell backward through the air, squinting her eyes shut as she braced herself for the pain of her head hitting the ground.

It never happened.

Instead, sturdy arms banded around her and caught her by the waist and shoulders, like a dancer in a Broadway show. Frankie opened her eyes in shock, looking straight up into blue orbs framed by silver wires. Dimly, she registered the crack of her helmet hitting the ground.

"Gotcha," Sam huffed. Time froze. His gaze dropped to her mouth. Her hands reached out of their own accord and wrapped around his neck. But before she could kiss her rescuer, he turned his head. "Next time you should take my hand."

A sunburned sensation bloomed across her face, neck and ears as he helped her get her feet under her again. He stood so close she could watch his Adam's apple bob as he gulped. "S-sorry," she stammered out.

"It's okay." He turned his head and ran a hand through his hair. "Well, let's get the tailgate up and we can get out of here. It's getting close to rush hour." Then he turned to do just that, leaving her to pick up her helmet and climb into the passenger side. Thankfully, Roger had installed a runner here so she could step up with ease.

It was going to be a long ride.

Chapter 8

THE AWKWARD SILENCE ON the way back to Roger's house gave Sam way too much time to think. Only the sound of the voice guidance on his phone accompanied them. Had he wanted her to kiss him? Fuck, yes. But the last thing he wanted was for her to do it out of obligation. So, as usual, he'd insulted her instead.

God, he was being such an ass. Everything just came out of his mouth wrong.

Well, he could at least make one thing right.

"I... I hope you will accept my apologies."

Frankie turned her head to look at him. "For what?"

Everything that comes out of my mouth?

He cleared his throat instead. "I should have locked the door last night. Nothing that happened last night was your fault."

She stared straight ahead. "Thank you. For that and for... catching me back there."

"You're welcome. I... I didn't mean to insinuate you were less than intelligent for not accepting my hand at first."

He had to keep his eyes on the road, but he wished he could see her expression. It took her a moment to respond, while sweat beaded on his forehead. "What do you mean?"

Sam tried to explain with a shrug. "You're independent and you wanted to try it without help first. I respect that. But the experiment showed that you needed help to get down. It just... came out wrong." *Like everything else I say to you*, he thought with a grimace.

"Oh."

They finished the drive in silence. Sam pulled the truck into the garage and put it in park. He waited at the garage door for Frankie to join him, then they walked across the yard and entered the house.

Roger looked up from his phone when they came in and hopped up from the couch. "Hey man, I got your note." He caught the keys when Sam tossed them to him.

"Do you know where I could get a new tire?" Frankie asked as she toed off her boots and left them by the door.

Roger nodded. "Caleb works at his dad's motorcycle shop. I've already texted him."

Just then, Jenna came down the stairs. "Hey, how was your ride?"

Frankie turned to her and snorted. "Great, until I blew a tire."

"Is your bike okay?"

"Yeah, I kept it upright." She shrugged. "I just hope all I need is a tire."

Roger's phone pinged with a text. "He says we can bring it over tomorrow."

"Sounds good."

"He wants to know what make and model you have." Roger handed Frankie his phone. "Go ahead and type it in."

She took the phone, and her thumbs flew over the keyboard. Roger eyed Sam, which told him he was staring at her. He glanced away, but he knew Roger would have questions the next time they were alone.

"I should probably get back to work." Sam wanted to finish that test and prepare the report for the client.

"You know, you're still on vacation. I don't expect you to work the whole time you're here."

He just shrugged. "We wanted a test run, right?"

"Yeah, but not the entire month." Roger gripped his shoulder. "I have a break between jobs coming up. I'll take you around to play tourist. Oh, and Mom wants us at dinner on Sunday."

"Your mom's been doing those family dinners a lot more often lately," Jenna murmured. "Is she okay?"

Roger shrugged. "She's struggling with Finn being overseas. On base in Okinawa, at least he could call home regularly. He can't from the sandpit. And all his other deployments came while he was stationed stateside. So it feels different."

Sam nodded. His mother had fretted constantly whenever he was on a mission, and she didn't have the fortitude Judy Hunt had. "Well, if Mama Hunt wants to feed us, the least we can do is show up."

Jenna and Roger nodded. Frankie looked like a deer in the headlights as she handed Roger back his phone. "I can't imagine she meant me."

"She knows you're staying with us." Jenna turned to her friend. "You've already met her. She was here when Caleb proposed to Nadia."

Frankie just blinked. "I met a lot of people that night, but I don't remember a single name."

"Nadia is my little sister. That whole thing was a setup for her boyfriend to pop the question. You came in right as dinner started." At her blank stare, Roger patted her on the shoulder. "You're welcome to join us. It won't be nearly as many people, and I'm happy to do introductions all over again."

"Never let anyone say that I turned down free food." Then she wrinkled her adorable round nose. "I hope she doesn't expect me to bring something I've made. I can't cook for shit."

Roger laughed. "She cooks enough for an army. She won't let us bring anything."

Frankie looked a little uncomfortable at that.

"I'll pick up some wine. How about that?" Sam suggested. To Roger, he said, "Do your parents drink wine?"

"Mom'll love that." Roger grinned.

"I'm going to get back to that test and run the report for you. I should be done soon." Sam nodded at the rest of them and headed for the stairs.

Roger called after him. "Then you're back on vacation mode!"

Sam shook his head and volleyed back, "What's that?"

FRANKIE STOMPED UPSTAIRS SHORTLY after Sam left the living room. Her ride had been doing her so much good, and then wham! She became more agitated than she'd been when she'd left. Now, instead of being frustrated over the lack of progress in discovering this cipher, she was worried about her bike. And irritated at herself for nearly kissing Sam, who clearly didn't want her. If he had, he wouldn't have pulled away.

Maybe short, curvy Black girls weren't his thing. Maybe he wasn't interested in a vacation fling. His loss, Frankie decided.

No. Frankie shook her head at herself as she neared the office door. There was no use thinking about hooking up with him. He was FBI, and she was a criminal. They might not be in his jurisdiction, but she was the hacker he'd been tasked to find, and Jenna was the reason. Even if she had the guts to expose herself like that, she wouldn't expose Jenna. They had to stick together or the syndicate would win. No hookup, no matter how hot he was, was worth that.

As she'd suspected, nothing had turned up in her search for the cipher on the hidden server. Which meant she had to go into the other servers to search for it and her haystack just got infinitely larger.

A thought occurred as Frankie sat down in her chair. What if the key for the code wasn't in the computers at all? That would make sense, right? Whoever was in on this part of the business might keep the addresses and the code off the computers to avoid one of the hackers finding it. The syndicate went to great lengths to keep their minions from knowing too much about each other. Keeping that server address, passwords, et cetera on paper would align with their paranoia.

But it made her job impossible.

She stared blankly at her screen, wondering which server she should start with. What to search for?

This wasn't her wheelhouse. This wasn't even in the same neighborhood.

Sighing, she reconnected to the syndicate's network and started looking at the files again.

Frankie realized she needed a new strategy. Looking for the file on the servers was getting her nowhere. If anyone had it digitized, they wouldn't leave it on a shared server. It would be on their personal computer.

Smirking, she cracked her knuckles. Time to get to work.

She started noting who had last edited the invoices, uploaded them, and when. While the usernames were random and senseless, she *had* to find a pattern. Once she figured out who was accessing things, that would tell her where she needed to focus.

Usernames lead to IP addresses, which showed her where to hack. That's when she really had to be careful. Someone poking around in a shared folder wouldn't be as noticeable as they would in a computer's hard drive. She steered clear of the targets whose computers showed they were actively in use. Only computers who had been idle for an hour or more were safe enough.

She was still looking for a needle in a haystack, but at least the stacks were smaller. And people didn't usually get too creative with filenames when they were only on their own computers.

Time quickly got away from her as she worked from this new angle. She wasn't sure how long Sam had been looking over her shoulder until he spoke. "Where did you learn to code?"

Damn the man. She could have sworn he lived to break her concentration. "I'm self-taught."

"This isn't any kind of coding I've ever seen before."

"Well, I'm not really coding here. I'm just searching for information."

"Seriously, where did you go to school?"

"Where did *you* go to school?" she asked in a mocking tone.

"I did my certifications through the Army."

Oh, the white boy was certified, was he? Frankie hadn't even finished high school. She'd learned early on how much more lucrative hacking and cryptocurrency was and dropped out.

It was easy to play the system when you knew how not to get caught. Fake credit cards got her through a lot before she ended up recruited by the syndicate.

Actually, now that she didn't have that meal ticket, she wondered for the first time how she was going to make her living. Identity theft was a lot harder to get away with these days. And Jenna was inspiring. Could Frankie give up crime altogether, too?

But what else could she do?

When Sam cleared his throat, she realized she'd gone too far down the rabbit hole and left him hanging. "I didn't go to school."

"What?" He sounded shocked, and when she turned to look at him, the aghast look made her want to laugh.

"I wasn't interested in the Army, and I certainly didn't have money for college. The library is free and has plenty of books." And access to computers. She crossed her arms over her chest and glared.

"So you're telling me you worked for this... organization, and you had no credentials?"

He really should close his mouth. The flies were going to get in.

"College isn't attainable for everyone, and it definitely wasn't necessary to do what I did. Do," she corrected herself. Ugh, did he have to loom over her like that? She hated being short.

"But a coder would need—"

Ugh. All her frustration came roaring forth. At her bike, at the time she had lost looking for the cipher, and at the hot-as-fuck Fed. "Look, if you don't want to help, then you're welcome to ignore me. But Roger and Jenna are willing and they're not questioning my methods. College, credentialing. All of it is bullshit and doesn't mean anything in the long run. Now, if you don't mind, my uneducated ass was on my way to a nice little breakthrough."

"Knock, knock." Both Sam's and Frankie's heads snapped to the door. Jenna stood there, leaning in the open space. "Frankie, why don't you come to dinner with me and Erin? We're having a girls' night."

All the wind went out of her sails. Frankie looked at her monitor, then at Sam, and back at Jenna. Damn it, she should stay and keep searching.

"The servers will still be there when we get back in a few hours."

She sighed. "Sure. Let me disconnect." She felt Sam's presence leave as he moved back to his desk.

"I'll let Erin know and order an Uber."

"An Uber?"

"Yeah, Nadia told me this place has margarita pitchers." Jenna grinned.

"Oh hell yes, foxy lady. I'm so there."

Chapter 9

FRANKIE SIGHED AS SHE slid into the dark wood booth in the restaurant, Fabled, and looked around. The bar in the middle looked like a tree that had fallen in a forest and sprouted taps. TVs on the walls showed various live streamed video games. Looking over the menu, she saw items like Hobbit's Pie, Elven Forest Salad, and a Necromancer Burger that said you had to sign a waiver when you ordered it. Even the cocktails were fantasy themed. Jenna hadn't given her long to change, but it was laid back so her jeans and "Computer whisperer" t-shirt fit right in. She'd had just enough time to pull her hair up into a poof before the rideshare pulled up.

An athletic woman with blonde curls slid into the booth across from her and Jenna.

"Roomie!"

"Hey, Amber." Her eyes shifted back and forth.

"Just Jenna now. It's fine."

"Really?"

"Yeah, I'll explain later. Erin, this is Frankie. Frankie, my former roommate, Erin."

Ah. The one who had been living with Jenna in the apartment the syndicate had ransacked.

"Nice to meet you." Frankie shook her hand across the table.

"Nice to meet you, too." Erin leaned into her seat. "God, I needed this."

"Everything okay?" Jenna asked.

Erin shrugged. "I'm exhausted. Between work, commuting by bus, and helping my parents out, I barely have time to sleep."

Their server popped up next to the table. "Welcome, ladies. Can I get you some drinks while you look over the menu?"

"Hold that thought, Erin," Jenna said. "Anyone want a specific margarita flavor for our first pitcher?"

"The peach looked good." Frankie licked her lips.

Erin leaned her chin on her hand. "Sounds fine to me."

"A pitcher of peach margaritas, please," Jenna gave their order to the server.

"Hang on a sec. Sir, what's your shirt say?"

The server looked down and grinned. "Home of the Necromancer Burger. So much spice it kills you twice!"

"Oh, my God!" Frankie covered her mouth as Erin and Jenna also suppressed giggles. "That's amazing."

He grinned. "We sell them up at the front desk. And there are glasses, too, if that's more your style."

"I'll think about it."

"Alright. Let me put this drink order in for you and then I'll let you get acquainted with our menu."

Jenna snickered. "I have to tell Nadia about those shirts."

"The girl that told you about this place?" Erin asked.

"Yeah, Roger's sister. Apparently, her fiancé tried one of the spicy burgers and couldn't handle it. I'd be willing to bet she'd buy him the shirt just to mess with him."

Frankie snorted. "I like the way you think."

"Now," Jenna crossed her arms on the table and leaned over them. "Why haven't you bought a new car, Erin?"

Erin hid behind her menu and sighed. "Because the landlord raised the rent and the money from the insurance company wouldn't go very far. I can't afford the higher rent as well as a car payment."

"I feel responsible, Erin. Why won't you let me help?"

"Because at the end of the day, it wasn't you who blew up my car. It was someone else." She glared at Jenna around the folder in her hands. "I'm doing okay. It's just tiring taking the bus everywhere."

"What about when you work overnights?" Their server had snuck up and silently dropped off the pitcher and three margarita glasses at their table before gliding away. Jenna started to pour and passed out glasses while they talked.

"I told my boss I wasn't available for a night shift for the foreseeable future."

"I can't imagine that went over well."

Erin sucked on her straw and gave a shiver. "Damn, that's good. Good call, Frankie."

Frankie nodded in agreement. "Thanks. I'm sorry, what do you do?" she asked Erin.

"I'm an emergency dispatcher. So I take 9-1-1 calls, send emergency services out, all that stuff."

Frankie raised her eyebrows but controlled her reaction otherwise. Damn, Jenna had been living with someone who worked for the police? Foxy had balls.

"What did your boss say?"

"He's not happy, but Gene happened to overhear. He made some comment about not putting the employees in a dangerous position and Harold grumbled but agreed." She sighed again. "Unfortunately, I thought I would be getting another car when we had that conversation. Now I'm not so sure."

"Can you borrow your parents'?"

"I might have to. But my insurance is going to be sky high because now the area I park in has that explosion on record." She rubbed a hand through her hair. "Honestly, I've been considering moving home, anyway. Between the rent and the car situation, something's gotta give."

"I'm so sorry, Erin."

That's when Frankie remembered something Jenna had told her when they'd reconnected. *The syndicate ransacked my apartment and blew up my roommate's car.* Holy shit, no wonder Jenna felt so guilty over it.

At that moment, their server arrived to take their orders. When it was Frankie's turn, she ordered the Mermaid's Bounty Pasta. Erin ordered the Elven Salad, and Jenna got some kind of chicken sandwich.

"How's Gene doing, by the way?" Jenna smirked.

Erin rolled her eyes. "We're not seeing each other, Jenna."

Oh, this sounded juicy. "Who's Gene?"

Jenna answered for Erin. "He's a detective who gives off major protective daddy vibes whenever Erin's around."

"Jenna! He does not."

"Even Roger could tell he has a thing for you."

Erin shook her curls. "Never going to happen. He's, like, fifteen years older than me."

Frankie decided to play devil's advocate. "Age ain't nothing but a number."

"Not you, too."

Jenna threw her hands in the air. "All I'm saying is if six feet, four inches of tattooed badass wanted to protect me, I'd be all over that."

"Girl, you already are." Frankie gave Jenna the side-eye.

The redhead snickered around her straw. "The detective has way more tattoos. And Roger is only six feet tall."

"How do you know that?" Erin scowled.

"Well, for one, because they go down to his knuckles."

The table was silent for a minute as their plates arrived. "My parents would flip a gasket," Erin admitted quietly.

"He treats you well, right?"

A blush rose over the blonde's cheeks. "I haven't dated him."

Frankie twirled pasta around her fork and watched the show. This was fun as hell. If Jenna had wanted to distract her, she'd succeeded.

"He wants to, doesn't he?" Jenna asked, taking a bite of her sandwich.

Erin shrugged. "If he wanted to, he'd have asked me out already. We've worked together for years, and he's never asked once."

"He probably thinks you'll say no."

"Because he's too old for me!" Erin cried. Then she poked at her salad again. "Plus, we work together. That would get awkward."

"But you told me yourself other people don't understand your crazy work hours."

"And if they do understand, we both have crazy schedules and there's a good chance we won't have any time together." Erin shook her head. "Leave it alone. Please, Jenna."

"Alright. For now. But someday the two of you are going to burst into flames and then you'll have to deal with it."

"You're entitled to your wrong opinion."

Frankie snorted.

"Speaking of combusting, what the hell was going on with you and Sam, Frankie?"

Great, now Jenna had focused her attention on her. "That man drives me absolutely batshit crazy. He's so rude. And he clearly doesn't think I know what I'm doing." She stuffed linguine in her mouth so she wouldn't have to keep talking.

Jenna's brow furrowed together as she looked thoughtful. "That's not the vibe I get at all. But okay."

"Really? What do you see?"

"I think he likes you."

Frankie snorted. "The man can't stand me." She tried not to think about the way she'd almost kissed him just earlier that day. Or how he'd obviously reacted to her when she accidentally walked in on him in the shower. It didn't matter, anyway. She didn't *do* love. It wasn't in her skill set. No one had ever shown her how. Her mother had loved heroin more than her own daughter. The foster families she got shuffled around to didn't love her, either. There was no point in getting attached to anyone because chances were she'd be leaving after a few months.

"Okay."

"What the hell? How come I get the third degree, and she gets acceptance?" Erin glared at Jenna.

"I've spent more time around Gene and you than I have Frankie and Sam. But don't worry," her sly friend said and winked. "I have a feeling that's going to change."

Lordy. Well, Frankie did not think it was going to go the way Jenna did. Erin scowled, mumbling something about unfairness, and then they moved on to other topics for the night.

She was glad she'd gotten out of the house, though. Despite Jenna stirring the pot, she really enjoyed girls' night out.

Chapter 10

THE CHIRP OF CRICKETS and the hoot of an owl greeted the rapidly descending night. Roger and Sam lounged on the back porch with cold beers and a comfortable silence only developed over years of friendship. Sam compared it to a much more tense silence between them back in their Army days. But here in Maryland there was no enemy pointing guns or laying roadside bombs. At least not yet.

Only bats hunting their evening meal while he and his friend sat together.

"Thanks for helping me out during your vacation." Roger took a sip from his bottle.

"Thanks for not giving up on me." Sam tipped his beer at his friend.

Roger smirked. "You shouldn't thank me for nagging you."

Sam shook his head. "You didn't nag me. I just wasn't ready to leave the Bureau yet."

His friend hummed. "You've always had a place on my team, brother. That's never going to change."

Sam smiled to himself. He hadn't had to wonder what it was like to have siblings, not since he joined the Army.

"Everything okay with you and Frankie?"

Sam lowered his gaze, unable to look Roger in the eye. "I don't understand where she fits in."

The wooden chair Roger sat in creaked as he shifted positions. "What do you mean?"

"You were Jenna's bodyguard, and she used to work with Frankie. But you never told me what Jenna used to do."

Now he'd made Roger uncomfortable. "It's not really my story to tell."

"That's fair." Damn it, he just kept putting his foot in his mouth tonight. "It's not really any of my business."

"But you want it to be."

Sam shook his head. "No, your girl is none of my business."

Roger shook his head. "What I meant was, you want to make Frankie your business."

Sam's chin fell to his chest. "She can't stand me."

"I can't help that you have no game." Now Roger was back to teasing him.

"You know that my only game was our uniform." He'd been far more comfortable behind a screen than talking to women. No one outside the Army had really understood all the technology that went into fighting these days, least of all his father. Dad had been an infantry guy, so while he'd been proud as hell that his son had made it into the Special Forces, he'd often scratched his head when Sam had tried to explain his actual job.

Roger pulled his feet from the railing and set them on the floor. "You can't tell me you haven't gotten laid since we retired."

Since before then, but Sam didn't have the heart to tell him that. He just let the silence speak for him.

"Man, I'm sorry." Roger took another swig from his beer. "I had no idea."

He didn't want to talk about it. "Forget about it. Even if I find her attractive, she doesn't want me. It's fine."

The silence hung heavily between them in the night air while the memory of how she'd felt in his arms assaulted Sam. How the daze in her deep brown eyes had softened them for a moment. Her hands on the back of his neck as she'd pulled herself up.

The idiocy with which he'd rejected the kiss he'd thought she was going to lay on him.

Even if she'd been doing it out of some misplaced desire to thank him for keeping her off the ground, he should have accepted it instead of being an ass.

He wanted to bang his head off the wall. What kind of idiot rejected a kiss he desperately wanted? Sam Ivers.

She'd never look his way again now.

Roger cracked his neck and stood from his chair. "Well, I got an early morning tomorrow. I better get going."

"Night."

"See you tomorrow."

Sam stayed outside to finish his drink, then went back inside the house. He didn't bother to turn the lights in the kitchen on, just locked the back door and went to the sink to rinse out his bottle. As he turned the water off, he heard the front door open with a bang.

"Shh! The boys are probably asleep."

"Sorry!" Giggling ensued from the foyer as Jenna and Frankie banged around, drunkenly taking their shoes off. Sam was about to announce himself and go upstairs, but then he heard his name.

"Seriously, though. He's such an elitist." That was Frankie. Sam hid in the shadows, eavesdropping, even though he knew he shouldn't.

"What do you mean?"

"I mean... he was asking where I went to college, Foxy. College! Can you imagine me in college?" More drunken giggles, punctuated by a few snorts.

"Where did you go to school, then?"

Their whispers were so loud, he wondered if Roger was listening as well.

"The University of Hard Knocks, bitch. I majored in fucking shit up."

Hard knocks? Sam's eyebrows furrowed. Then the meaning dawned on him. That's how he'd offended her.

Well, shit.

"Come on, let's get upstairs."

"You just want to jump your man."

"Can you blame me?"

A pause. "Nah. I'm happy for you. But I'm still going to tease you."

Frankie sounded like the alcohol was running its course. Sam waited until their footsteps faded from the ceiling before sneaking a peek into the hall.

Deserted.

He crept back to the kitchen, filled a glass with water and slipped up the stairs on silent feet. The door to Frankie's room was shut, as he expected. He pushed open his door and headed for the bathroom. Thankfully that was open. Leaving the glass on her side of the sink, Sam found the aspirin in the medicine cabinet and left it out next to the drink. Then he locked her door for a few minutes, did his business, and brushed his teeth. Unlocking it again, he shut the light off and closed the door to his room.

Laying in his borrowed bed, Sam stared at the ceiling while thinking about what he'd overheard. Was he really that elitist? He'd grown up in a stereotypical suburban neighborhood with two parents, one of whom was deployed a good bit when he was young, but he remembered his dad being around more often than not. His mother had been a teacher, so she valued education above all else.

"I don't care if you're in the Army, you need to get your degree!"

So he earned his bachelor's in computer science one class at a time, around his deployments and training. When he'd finally finished, there had been no commencement ceremony, just a night out at the bar with the guys before they had to report the next morning.

But Mom had been satisfied. And when he got out of the military, he had a career all set up.

Sam had never thought of himself as anything other than normal, but Frankie's comments had him wondering what happened to her as a child. What had she lived through? Again, she was a puzzle he yearned to solve.

More than that, he wanted to get to know Frankie. They could have so much in common with their line of work. Not for the first time, the question of how she got wrapped up in an organization that dabbled in human trafficking crossed his mind, but he dismissed it. People like that hid their evil deeds until you stumbled across them, tripped, and fell flat on your face. He didn't have any first-hand experience like Frankie apparently did, but he'd heard plenty from coworkers, and watched enough true crime shows with Roger back in the barracks to know it was the truth.

Sam set his glasses on the nightstand and sat up to pull his shirt off over his head. He left his clothes on the floor by the bed and laid back down under the covers, rubbing a hand over the hollow feeling in his chest. There was no point thinking too hard about it now. Besides, she wasn't a Rubik's Cube. She was a person with feelings. Now if he could just keep his foot out of his mouth.

Chapter 11

FRANKIE HAD HER FINGERS buried in Sam's curls, his tongue driving her to new heights. She should have known there was a better use for his mouth.

They were naked in her apartment, her legs spread-eagle on her mattress as he ate her out like he'd never get enough.

She moaned and gushed like a porn star until finally she pulled his head up. It wasn't enough.

"Fuck me, already."

"Say please." The asshole smirked as he lined himself up.

Frankie rolled her eyes. Even in her dreams, he was full of himself.

Wait. Even in her dreams?

With that, Frankie's eyes snapped open. Sunlight streamed through the window, blinding her momentarily and making her squint as her brain came online. Well, it tried to. Too many margaritas from the night before had her mouth feeling like it was filled with cotton and her head like little men were jack hammering away inside. She rolled off the air mattress and stumbled to the bathroom.

Inside, she discovered someone had left a tall glass of water and the aspirin on her side of the sink. Either Jenna had gotten up earlier than her, or Drunk Frankie was smarter than she thought. She downed the painkiller, then chugged the water. It woke her up enough to remember to lock Sam's door before she sat on the toilet. At least Drunk Frankie had remembered her bonnet. Otherwise, her hair would be a mess.

Could Sam have brought her the water? Jenna wouldn't want to disturb either of them, and chances were she was feeling the tequila this morning, too. Either way, it was a sweet gesture. Hopefully, the painkiller kicked in soon.

She had hunting to do.

Two hours, three slices of toast and an enormous cup of coffee later, Frankie sat down at her desk. She fired up her laptop and sat back. Scrubbing a hand over her eyes once it connected, she opened the next location on the list.

Even with the assistance of tequila, she'd barely slept the last few nights. When Dream Frankie wasn't sexing up a certain blonde Fed, nightmares about how she continually failed the victims of the of the syndicate plagued her. To be honest, the Russian roulette was getting old.

Sam had been subdued in the kitchen that morning, his words measured. Not only did she suspect the water and aspirin on her side of the sink *had* been his doing, but he'd apologized for upsetting her. Again.

The man was somehow both infuriating and alluring at the same time. No wonder her poor libido was confused.

Paging through another email account, careful to leave everything marked unread when she was done, Frankie squinted at her screen. All she needed was one piece of the puzzle, one bread crumb that would lead her to the next.

This guy was no low-level peon. She wasn't familiar with his code name, but he was definitely higher up the food chain than she'd been. And this was in his sent folder.

> **Hey Marcus,**
>
> **You said you were interested in acquiring a certain product. Information regarding these auctions is only available in person at events. I can't go to this one below, but I can get you on the list if you want. Ask for...**

Frankie scanned the information, and the hair on the back of her neck stood straight up. This was it. It had to be. Marcus, whoever he was, had declined the invitation, saying he wasn't available either, but Frankie copied the email before she shut the connection to the syndicate servers down. A quick search showed her the event itself was legit, but they would need tickets and to find the contact. Frankie printed out the information on Roger's printer and ran downstairs.

Roger met her at the bottom. "I was just coming up to get you. Caleb said to bring the bike over today, remember?"

"Bike... right!" Her motorcycle! How could she forget she'd busted a tire just yesterday? "Uh, I have news."

"Did you find something?"

"Yes..." Frankie winced. Her poor bike needed TLC. Next to her computer, that thing was her baby. "I guess the new information can wait?"

"Jenna!" Roger hollered.

"What?" Foxy appeared with a raised eyebrow, unamused.

"Frankie has news."

"I don't want to keep your sister's boyfriend waiting..." Frankie chewed on her lip.

"Did you find the cipher?" Sam emerged from the open basement door.

He wore a gray t-shirt soaked in sweat and he chugged from a water bottle as that intense blue stare lasered in on her. So that's what he did first thing in the mornings. Frankie tore her gaze away as she answered. "No, not yet. I don't think they're keeping it on the servers. The information I found mentioned an auction and that the information was only available in person, so I assume we have to be there."

"But we don't know where 'there' is." Jenna took another sip of her coffee.

"I mean, I found where to go to get that information. One of us has to go to this gala." She produced the sheet she'd printed out with the original email. She handed it to Roger while Jenna came over to look over his shoulder.

"A gala?" asked Sam.

"Yeah, all we need is a way in. I got the name of the syndicate contact who will be there. We have to find him to get the auction information."

"Are we sure that's what they're discussing in this email?" Roger looked skeptical.

Frankie shrugged. "It's the best lead I've got. Worst-case scenario, we go to the auction and it turns out to be art or something legitimate."

"No, worst-case scenario, we end up detained for crashing a party." Jenna looked from Roger to Frankie and back again.

Right. Jenna was reminding her that they could end up dead, but she didn't want to say anything in front of Sam.

"Sam, I know you're not interested in fieldwork, but these people already know who I am and what I look like. Not to mention Jenna. It'll have to be you."

She hadn't thought it possible for Sam to get any paler. "Are you shitting me right now?"

"Unfortunately, no."

"I can't possibly—"

"Please, Sam? We don't have any other leads."

"I'm not going alone."

One by one, they all turned to Frankie. "M-m-me?" Her heart pounded as her stomach dropped. "You want *me* to go to a fancy freakin' gala?"

Concern and worry painted Jenna's face. "I would go if I could, but I'm too well known. What if someone from my father's world recognizes me? We'd be dead in the water."

"It's three days away!" And the other reason she didn't want to voice was, *"No one is going to believe we're an item."*

Sam clutched his water bottle as his face turned red. "Frankie, you're so much better in social situations than I am. I will freeze and I refuse to waste this chance." His

Adam's apple bobbed as he gulped. "It would be better to have four eyes on the case rather than two. That way, if things go sideways, we have a chance of one of us getting away and getting help." He licked his lips and the pathetic way he asked the next word sealed her fate. "Please?"

Damn. She really couldn't turn him down now. This was her pet project, anyway. The faces from those photographs flashed before her when she closed her eyes, and Frankie took a deep breath.

"Guess we better find a dress after we get my bike fixed."

Sam's color slowly returned to normal. "How do you propose we get in?"

Frankie rubbed her hands together. Now was her time to shine. "Option one: I email the contact while impersonating this Marcus fellow, say my situation changed, and ask him to add me and my date to the list."

Roger rubbed his chin. "The only problem is when our target sees Marcus or talks to him and asks how the gala went. Or what if they want photo ID?" He shook his head. "Too many ways for that to go wrong."

She'd thought of that, too. That's why she preferred option two.

"Option two, Sam and I dress up as janitors and go in early, then change while inside and enter the party from within the building."

"That's still risky. We don't know if they have cleaning staff already." Sam pointed out.

"Well, if that fails, there's always option three."

Sam tilted his head to the side. "What's option three?"

Frankie shrugged. "Wait until the party is in full swing, then hack the backdoor and sneak in that way. I'd need a blueprint of the building and some information on their security system, but I have enough time."

Sam's eyes narrowed, but he didn't speak his suspicious thoughts out loud.

"I think that's the safest plan," Roger said, "but we can do the janitorial one if it doesn't look like it will work."

She gave him a nod. "I'll work on getting the building specs once we get home."

"Alright. I'll drive you over to Gray Customs so Caleb can fix your bike."

"I'm coming, too." Jenna said. "Not only am I going nuts in this house, but I want to help Frankie find a dress."

Frankie groaned. "I didn't even think about that. I don't know if we can find a gown to fit all this ass in three days."

"Your ass is awesome. Now let's go." Jenna sauntered toward the front door.

"I never said it wasn't. It's just hard to find clothes for." She started to follow, but turned when Sam spoke.

"Guess I better come, too." Sam shrugged. "I didn't exactly plan on this, so my suit is at home."

Jenna eyed Sam up and down, and Frankie had to hold back a glare. Jenna wouldn't ever flirt with someone else in front of her man. "Could you borrow one of Roger's?"

Sam and Roger looked at each other, and Roger shrugged. "It might work. But I need to take Frankie over to Gray like, now. So why don't I do that and then we can come back for you two?"

"Works for me. I'll raid your closet in the meantime." Sam drained his water bottle and headed for the recycling bin in the kitchen. "I'll text with an update."

Chapter 12

WHAT THE HELL HAD he gotten himself into? Sam scrubbed a hand down his face as he climbed the stairs. Not only was he willingly headed into a potentially unstable situation, but there would also be a lot of innocent people around them that would expect him to socialize.

He hadn't had any other option but to beg Frankie to go with him. There was no way Sam could pull this off by himself. It had been too long since he did ops in the Army, and he was definitely no James Bond.

Roger's only suit sat in its drycleaning bag in the very back of the closet. Sam pulled it out and went to lay it on Jenna and Roger's bed, but decided to take it back to the guest room to change. He did have one collared shirt with him, thank goodness, so he pulled that out of the suitcase and changed his clothes.

Looking in the mirror, he felt like he was wearing an older brother's hand-me-down. Roger's shoulders were broader than Sam's, and his legs longer. Sam shook his head and changed back into his jeans and t-shirt. He hung the suit back up and put the bag over it once more, then shot a text to Roger that he'd need to go shopping as well. Roger sent back a thumbs-up emoji. Satisfied his friend would come back for him, he hung his dress shirt up in the guest room closet, then replaced Roger's suit in his own.

Downstairs, Sam picked up the email Frankie had printed out again and searched for the gala on his phone. Black tie, so he'd need to find a tuxedo rental. Then he noticed the venue. It was at a hotel.

That was perfect. He could rent a room, and then he and Frankie could just sneak down once the event was underway. And since it was bound to be a late night, they could just stay in the room and not worry about tipping anyone off.

Why the hell hadn't *she* thought of that?

Sam scratched his head. There was no need to break into anything. The only issue was, could they get tickets for this thing?

When he looked at the site further, he saw "Sold Out" listed under the ticket sales page. Damn. So they would still have to sneak, but at least they wouldn't be breaking and entering.

Why would she go straight to "let's commit a felony" when looking for a solution?

The conversation he'd overheard between Jenna and Frankie came back to him. The School of Hard Knocks, indeed. He rubbed at the ache trying to bloom behind his forehead and looked for a distraction.

Sam busied himself with a book while waiting for them to return. Roger had put his foot down and forbid Sam from doing any more work during his vacation, outside of their minor operation, anyway. After a couple of hours, he heard a revving engine turn down the driveway, then slow immediately once it hit the gravel. Behind it, he heard Roger's truck. When the engines turned off, he slipped into his shoes and opened the front door. "How'd you make out?"

Frankie lifted her helmet and shook out her curls. "Just needed the tire. All good, now." She tucked the helmet under her arm and strode for the door. "I need to change my shoes before we go dress shopping."

"About the gala," he started, and she paused on the porch stairs, "it's at a hotel. Why don't I just book a room and we sneak in after they stop taking tickets? As long as we don't take anyone's seat at the dinner, we should go unnoticed."

"Simple. I like it." She slipped past him into the house, where she bent over to unzip her boots. Her plush round bottom up in the air gave him some dirty ideas, and he quickly averted his eyes.

"I'm surprised you didn't suggest that first."

"I just didn't think of it. It makes way more sense."

"Plus, we'll just be guests at the hotel. We can stay the night and then leave in the morning."

"You want to be in a hotel room with me?" The look on her face said it all.

He shrugged. "We're supposed to be pretending to be on a date. Why would we get two rooms?"

"You're right," she said with a groan. Then put her hands on her hips. "You don't snore, do you?"

"Not that I'm aware of."

"Good."

Two days later, Sam returned from a run with Roger and hopped into the shower. He let the hot water relax his tense muscles as the steam fogged up the glass enclosure. The gala coming up had taken up the bulk of his mental capacities and he hadn't gotten much accomplished since the decision to go had been made. Not for the first time, he tried to consider if taking Frankie was smart. He'd meant what he said about needing someone more outgoing on the case, and that two sets of eyes were better than one, but was he just being selfish? Was he just trying to force her to spend time with him?

He finished his shower with no answer to his questions. After he dried himself off, he wrapped the towel around his waist and pulled out his shaving kit. Mom would kill him if he showed up to this gala scruffy, and his beard was too thick to get through it in one pass, so he'd do the first one now, and the next the day of the event. He wiped the fog from the mirror and sprayed the foam into his hand when Frankie's door opened.

"Oh. Morning."

"Good morning," he answered, glancing at the shaving cream filling his hand. "Sorry, did you need in here?"

"Just to brush my teeth," she replied.

He squeezed over and motioned for her to go ahead. "We can share."

She gulped audibly, and Sam struggled to focus solely on his face in the mirror.

"You're... in a towel."

He stole a glance at her and noticed her eyeing him up and down, blatant appreciation in her gaze. Sam's spine straightened and his chest puffed slightly. "Which is more than I was wearing last time."

Her cheeks darkened. Was that a blush? It was hard to tell. But when she turned sideways to pull down her toothbrush, he could see her nipples jutting out against her thin sleep shirt. She liked what she saw. Sam forced his eyes into the mirror and focused on the task at hand. Getting turned on in his state of undress could undo all the goodwill he'd just fostered.

Unfortunately, small talk was not his forte. And he still felt guilty on some level for dragging her to the gala when she hadn't seemed to want to go. "I'm sorry for dragging you to this gala, you know. I... I freaked out. I'm not good with people." Ugh, he hated showing his vulnerable underbelly like this. But he couldn't explain it any other way. "If you really want to back out, I can go it alone."

"It seems like you're always apologizing to me," she said around her toothbrush. Pulling it out, she waved it at him like a baton while he watched them in the mirror, his razor gliding over his jaw. "First, after I thought about it, you're right. No one would go to this thing stag, especially not a dude. So you'd stick out like a sore thumb. Second, you just surprised me, that's all." She returned to brushing her teeth and then rinsed her mouth as Sam patted his face dry.

"I didn't go to any dances in high school." Why the hell had he said that?

"Me either. I didn't really like high school boys."

"No one does. Not even other high school boys." He chuckled.

She put her toothbrush and toothpaste away slowly, bringing down some kind of facial cleanser and setting up shop on the sink. He ran a hand through his damp hair. Sam knew he shouldn't linger.

"See you downstairs." Sam nodded and slipped back into his room, shutting the bathroom door behind him.

He fought the urge to smack his head against the wall. Frankie would hear it and then she'd really think he was crazy.

But she was attracted to him. After all this time thinking there was nothing there, Sam realized he'd been wrong. This gala, he realized, was his chance to sweep her off her feet. To show her who he was under this awkward first layer.

The answer came a few hours later when Jenna and Roger were arguing over the movie Jenna wanted to watch that afternoon.

"It's a classic!"

"Princess, it's not even Thanksgiving yet!"

"So? It's my favorite."

Sam just chuckled. "I'll watch the Christmas movie with you, Jenna." He'd smirked, knowing Roger would cave, even if Sam would never make a move on someone else's girl.

Frankie had never seen *White Christmas*, and while Sam watched Danny Kaye sing about the best things happening while dancing, it clicked. He better brush up on his footwork.

Chapter 13

Frankie smoothed down the back of her short dress as she emerged from the bathroom. Wine red sequins glittered from her shoulders to her mid-thigh, and down both arms. With the fall evenings getting cooler, she'd opted for the long-sleeved cocktail dress with the plunging V-shaped neckline that clung to her curves and showed her girls off in all their glory. The gold clutch and strappy heels clinched the deal.

Sam made a choking sound.

Frankie's cheeks heated, and she eyed him carefully. "Need the Heimlich?"

He shook his head, his blonde curls not moving. *Hair gel,* Frankie thought with amusement. Guys were so lucky. They had it easy. Meanwhile, she'd spent two hours at a salon for a silk press, getting her hair all smooth and silky, curling at the ends like an old Hollywood starlet. And also getting a lecture on Black hair care from the stylist. She hadn't grown up in a Black family like most did, and it just wasn't a priority when she barely left her apartment back in Las Vegas. But she'd wanted to look her absolute best for this gala for some reason. Okay, she knew the reason, and he was standing in front of her. She'd even left her hair in the bonnet all day so he wouldn't see the full effect until she was ready.

"No, no, it's just... you're gorgeous."

Now she *knew* she was blushing, and she shrugged off his compliment, looking away. She swallowed as she took in his appearance in the mirror behind him. He filled out that suit perfectly.

"Think they stopped taking tickets yet?"

He nodded, those blue orbs unable to look away. "Yeah, according to their itinerary online, we're well past dinner now."

They'd eaten at an outside fast-food place so they wouldn't see anyone from the event. Then they'd come back to the hotel to change.

"What's the plan?" She slipped past him to grab her clutch and put her lipstick inside.

"We go down to the first floor and wander around. I have the blueprint from the county safety building on my phone, and the ballroom the gala is in has a few backdoors for staff."

"Sounds perfect."

They rode the elevator in silence, but just before the doors opened on the first floor, Sam offered her his arm.

"Shall we?"

Right. She was supposed to be his date.

Sam led her away from the noise of the main ballroom, and they slipped down some hallways. At first, they pretended they were looking for a bathroom, and then they went further into the back halls where it was deserted. Sam kept up the pretense, carefully glancing at his phone to check they were going in the right direction.

Eventually, their rouse worked. "Are you looking for the gala?" asked an employee dressed in a white and black server's uniform.

"Yes! We got a little lost." Frankie told her, acting her part.

"Come through here." The server gestured at a side door. "Your room is the next one over."

"Thank you." Sam nodded as they entered a short hallway where the sounds of a band could be heard. The door at the end let them out into a shadowed corner inside the ballroom.

Frankie took a moment to look around. A big crystal chandelier dazzled above the dance floor. People dressed to the nines roamed the room, schmoozing among the round tables scattered with forgotten silverware and glasses. A few couples danced to the tune the four-piece band played.

"What was the name of our contact, again?"

"Neil Farid."

Sam gestured to the name cards. "We're going to be hunting for a while."

She shook her head. "Do you think there's a seating chart?"

"It's not likely it's still up."

"Good point." With a sigh, she turned to her date for the evening. "We'd cover more ground if we split up."

His gaze took her in from head to toe once more. "Too dangerous. I wish we had a photo of this guy."

She shrugged. "We don't know if Neil is his real name."

He squared his shoulders and started circling the table slowly. Frankie grabbed onto his elbow once more. They meandered through the tables, stopping every so often and pretending to be deep in conversation. They'd discussed strategy on the way over to the hotel. Sticking to the shadows would keep them safe. It would be better to get the information and get out without drawing attention to themselves.

They paused by the bar, taking the opportunity to deflect suspicion by waiting in line for a drink. But that was when Frankie noticed the people in line had tickets they were exchanging for their beer and wine. Shit. That would give them away for sure.

She turned to Sam. "Darling, we left our drink tickets at the table."

With an apology, Sam and Frankie left the line.

Looking for this guy was like looking for a needle in a haystack all over again. Frankie led Sam toward the front door. There, cleaning up a ticket table, was someone who looked like they must be in charge.

"Stay here," Frankie whispered to Sam, who nodded. If she got kicked out of the event, one of them needed to find this Neil guy.

"Pardon me — Hayley," Frankie skimmed the nametag on the woman's blouse. "Do you have the seating chart handy? My friend and I were planning to meet up at the event, but I'm not sure what table they're at."

"Oh sure. Who are you looking for?"

"Neil Farid."

Hayley hummed as she flipped through papers on a clipboard. "He's on the left side of the room. Table eight."

"Thank you so much!" She swiftly ducked back into the ballroom, headed for the opposite side from where they'd come in. She'd nearly forgotten Sam until he tugged at her elbow.

"Slow down, Frankie." His murmur tickled her ear and sent shivers down her back.

"Sorry." Her breathing, harsher than she'd realized, made her bosom heave as she turned to face him. His glance downward didn't escape her notice. "I'm a grown woman, you know. You don't have to hold on to me the whole time."

"That's where you're wrong." His blue eyes blazed down at her. "You're exquisite and breathtaking, like a work of art that draws the eye of everyone. I have to hold on to you because if I don't, someone is going to think they can make off with you. But I want them to know that you're here with *me*." His pale hand gently cupped her chin and tilted her face up to look at him.

Frankie's heart pounded in her chest. The noise of the guests in the ballroom faded away until all she heard was her pulse keeping time with the music.

Sam drew his face close to her ear. "Table eight is empty," he murmured.

"Damn it." Sam's hold on her chin loosened, and then she felt his arms draw around her.

"Dance with me?"

Frankie blinked in surprise. Sam could dance? Letting him lead her onto the dance floor, she turned to look at table eight, but he stopped her.

"I'll keep watch, I promise. But we need to blend in."

Frankie nodded and found herself drawn into a simple sway side to side, her left hand on his shoulder, her right hand held in his, and his powerful arm banded around her back. She craned her head upward to look at him with fresh eyes. His passionate outburst had floored her. As they danced pressed against each other, the tension between them thickened. Frankie could have sworn it was a tangible entity in the room.

And then the beat changed. The band slipped into the dark sensual beats of a tango. When Frankie tried to pull away, Sam held her tighter, slipping his knee between her legs, sharpening his elbow into what she assumed was the proper tango posture. She raised an eyebrow in question.

"I used to take ballroom lessons," he said with a tilt to his lips.

"For real?" asked Frankie.

"Yes. My mother thought it would help me make friends. "

"Your mom sounds… interesting," Frankie replied.

"She has never fully been in touch with social trends."

"How old were you?"

"Between the ages of ten and twelve," he replied. "Young enough to think she might have a good idea, but old enough to know better than to tell the other kids at school," he said with a shy grin.

"And you still remember how to do this?"

"Let's find out. Follow my lead. Slow, slow, quick, quick slow." Sam demonstrated the steps and led her around the dance floor. Other couples vacated until only a handful remained. Step by step, turn by turn, Sam drew Frankie into a spiral of seduction.

"Aren't you supposed to look at the side when you tango?" she asked.

Sam's responding smile had devastating consequences for her underwear. "It might not be the correct form, but I can't look away from you."

All thoughts of what they had come here to do fled her mind. Frankie's vision went dark around the edges until all she could see was Sam. All she could hear was the crescendo of the music as the band played on. She couldn't tear her eyes away from her dance partner. The music had transformed him. And her, as well.

No one in her life had ever made Frankie feel so special. And when the band played the last note, Sam dipped her and pulled her back up to a thunderous applause. Blinking, the ballroom and the other guests came into view for her again. Sam's pale face was flushed with exertion, or maybe something else. She couldn't be sure. Yet again, the moment was perfect as his lips drew near. She wondered if this would be the moment he kissed her.

"Bravo!" A dark-haired man clapping his hands approached them, and Sam pulled back, visibly startled. Damn it, foiled again! The stranger was only a couple of inches taller than Frankie, so Sam towered over him. "That was delightful to watch," said the man. "Is it true that you were looking for me?" He raised an eyebrow in question, looking back and forth between them.

Frankie's brain came back online. "Are you Neil?"

He bowed. "I am. But who are you?"

Beside her, Sam cleared his throat. "We are friends of Andre. " That was the name to mention given in the email, Frankie remembered.

This seemed to be the code word that Neil was looking for. He nodded and slipped a card into Sam's hand as they shook.

"I wish you good health. Have a great rest of your night," Neil said. Sam slid the card into his pocket and nodded. The music changed to some upbeat cover, and Sam led Frankie off the dance floor in the opposite direction from where Neil was walking.

"So much for blending into the woodwork," said Frankie.

"On the contrary, I don't know that we would have gotten Neil's attention any other way."

"I guess you have a point." Frankie's pulse still thundered in her ears, and she was sure her makeup was melting.

"Did you want to stay?" Sam drew her back into his embrace like he couldn't keep his hands off her. And Frankie found she liked it a little too much. But he'd been the one to light this fire in her, and she needed him to put it out.

All night long.

"We have what we came for." Her black curls swayed as she shook her head. Then she lifted herself on her toes and pressed her hand over his firm chest. "I have other ideas of how we could spend the time."

His nostrils flared and one hand dropped to her hip and pressed her into him. There was no mistaking how he felt when his dick probed her belly. "Then let's get out of here."

They exited through the front door of the ballroom and into the hallway. Some of the actual guests stood around with drinks in their hands. They paid the pair no mind as they made a beeline for the elevators and the privacy of their hotel room.

Chapter 14

Sam's throat constricted as they strode down the hall to their room, as though he were a leashed wolf. He'd known as soon as he got his hands on her curves that he'd be a goner. What surprised him, was how eager she was when up until a day ago, he could have sworn she felt nothing for him but loathing. Perhaps this attraction hadn't been as one-sided as he'd thought.

Frankie's hands pulled at his buttons before he'd even thrown the deadbolt. Thank goodness he'd put the Do Not Disturb sign facing outward on their doorknob. No more damn interruptions tonight.

Or tomorrow morning.

He grabbed her hands to still them as his tie became her next casualty. "Frankie, Frankie, you're going out of order," he tsked, slowly tugging her hands back against the door, above her head.

Her brown gaze drank him in. "What are you talking about?"

He leaned over her, not as far as he normally would, given her heels. "We were interrupted down there."

Those plump lips lifted on one side in a painted dark red smirk. "We were?"

"Mmhmm." One palm kept her hands at bay, while the other tilted her chin upward. "I am dying to kiss you."

She sighed and leaned her head back further, her mouth parting. "About damn time."

He chuckled, then drew closer, pausing to run his nose down hers. Her breath puffed against his heated cheek. It had been so long since Sam felt an attraction to anyone, much less the all-consuming obsession he had for Frankie. Despite never being with a Black woman, he believed that beauty transcended race. And he'd *never* been so drawn to anyone before. Maybe it was because he'd never met someone with her unique combination of sass and tech knowledge before. She had that self-taught streetwise fire, and he was the trained operative with military precision. They complimented each other.

And when their lips finally met, the desire rocketed through his veins. A groan resonated in his throat and that's all it took for her to open her lips to him and stroke her tongue along his.

His upper hand released her wrists, joining the other to cup her face and angling it to deepen their kiss. Her fingers tangled in his hair, clutching at the gelled strands as she moaned into his mouth. When he finally came up for air, they were both gasping.

"Sam," she said between pants. "If. You don't. Fuck my brains out. This instant..."

He slammed his mouth back on hers and lifted her in his arms. Sam walked the ten steps to the closest queen-sized bed and laid her down, not letting his mouth leave hers until her back was on the mattress and her hands above her head. He pulled back and held them there with one hand while the other pulled his tie off his neck.

"I'll fuck you, sweetness. But it's going to be on *my* timetable." With some of the fastest knots he'd made since his days in the Army, he tied her hands together. Slipping a finger under the binding to make sure it wouldn't hurt her, he gave her a gentle smile. "Is this okay with you?"

Her dilated pupils and heaving breasts said her body was all in, even if her mind was unsure. "I... I've never..."

"I won't hurt you. I just want to worship you the way you deserve." He punctuated his meaning by sliding a hand up her skintight dress and caressing the curve of her naked ass.

Naked ass?

"What are you wearing under here?"

"A thong."

"How attached are you to it?"

"It matches the bra, so I'm pretty attached." Damn, he loved her sass.

Tugging at her binding again to taunt her, he raised both brows. "I'm still waiting for an answer, Frankie. Are you good with the tie?"

She closed her eyes for a moment, then opened them again. "Yes. And you can call me by my full name if you want."

"What do you mean?"

Her pink tongue darted out and licked at her lips, dark red smudges all around her mouth. "It's short for Francesca."

"That's beautiful." He ran the backs of his fingers down her cheek, in awe of this gift of trust. "You looked like a Francesca tonight."

"Looked?"

"Yes. Now you look like you're ready to be thoroughly debauched." He swept her dress up over her head and left it around her wrists, leaning forward to speak in her ear. "You look like *mine*." He grinned when she shivered and goose bumps erupted.

Jesus Christ. Seeing all that cocoa skin glistening in the light left him speechless. His fingers traced over her round breasts bursting to get out of her black lace bra, trailed over her thick belly, and then danced over her heavenly hips where the tiny scrap of black lace she wore over her sex barely kept her decent. Just a good strong tug on those straps and he'd tear the offending fabric right off her.

But then she'd be mad, and he couldn't have that. Moving to one side, he slid a finger between her legs.

"Oh sweetness, is all that honey for me?" Frankie whined and thrashed, trying to get him to apply more pressure before he was ready. "Patience, sweetheart." He slid his hands back over her in wonder. "You're so beautiful. I hardly know where to start."

"I have an idea for you."

"Ah, ah, ah. I told you it's going to be on my timeline. I have so many ideas. So many things I want to do to you."

First, he slipped a hand under her back and released her bra, sliding it up to sit with her dress above her head. Those luscious breasts burst free of their confinement, their tight brown nipples calling for his mouth. But first, he filled his hands with them, massaging and appreciating them. Then he brought his mouth down to one and licked over the mound. When she whimpered, he sucked the tight bud into his mouth and played with the other at the same time.

"Sam!"

He switched sides, her wet nipple easier to roll as his tongue flicked over the other. When she bucked her hips, he drew his hand down over her belly, tracing around her navel, then down, down, to her sopping wet core.

"You're drenched, sweetness. You need me?"

"Yes! Damn it, yes!"

Sam couldn't help but laugh. "Alright." Grinning, he went to his knees at the foot of the bed, pulling her ass to the edge. Then he gripped the sides of her panties and pulled the wet fabric off her hips and drew it down her legs.

"Why are you still dressed?" she asked.

"Are you sure you want me to remedy that right now?" He raised one eyebrow as he pressed on her thighs.

Huffing, she fought against his hands. "At least let me see you without a shirt on. I didn't get a good look that time in the shower."

"As you wish." He stood, making sure she could see him as he stuffed her underwear into his pants pocket and unbuttoned his dress shirt. Her murmur of approval as he slid the crisp cotton down his shoulders made him flex for her.

"Get in me, soldier boy."

"All in good time." He kneeled once more as she protested. "You see, I ordered room service. And it's just arrived."

Sam took the feet still wrapped in those sexy gold sandals that reminded him of a Greek goddess and placed them over his shoulders. Her protest faded to whimpers as he pressed open-mouthed kisses up her inner thighs, alternating sides. Then he locked his gaze on hers as he took his first lick up her slit. Her flavor burst on his tongue, and he dove in like the sex-starved man he was.

Her plush ass filled his hands as he licked and sucked at her honeypot. Frankie pulled his face right where she wanted it, squeezing her legs and digging her heels into his shoulders. Fuck, yes.

"Need... need..." she moaned and gasped. Sam had an idea of what his Frankie needed. No, *Francesca*. Mmm, that sounded delicious even in his head. Without preamble, he thrust two fingers into her delicious pussy while he sucked her clit into his mouth and flicked his tongue over it double-time. He fucked her with his fingers until she screamed, her climax clenching her muscles around his hand. When she'd come back down from heaven, he pulled out his fingers and met her eyes while he licked them clean. She shuddered with another aftershock.

Then he let her watch as he stood and stripped off his belt and pants, pausing to get a condom from his wallet before they fell to the floor. He kicked off his shoes and socks, then let her get a good long look at his cock before sliding the rubber on.

He nearly blew his load when she licked her lips. "Later," he promised. Then he lifted her legs again and bent her knees back to her tits, pausing to pet the mounds for a moment. Sam positioned his hands on either side of her head, staring into her eyes, dark pools that he would gladly drown in. Then, inch by inch, he slid home.

He took a moment to throw his head back and close his eyes, savoring the bliss of her heat. Then he brought his chin down to look at her once more. "Are you ready, Francesca?"

Chapter 15

SAM HAD RUINED HER for all other men with that kiss before he'd even taken her clothes off, so she knew fucking him was going to blow her mind. And no one had gone down on her like *that* before. If they did go down, it was just a stop on the way to their actual destination. Guys, she'd learned, were usually more concerned with getting their dick wet.

Now, finally, he was inside her. Frankie reveled in the sensation of being full. With her legs up like this, he was deeper inside her than anyone had ever been. With her hands bound, she discovered that the pleasure was even stronger, her focus solely on the places where he touched her.

"I've been ready."

They stared into each other's eyes as he slowly pulled back, then thrust inside her once more. A bead of sweat rolled down his forehead, along his straight Anglican nose, and splashed between her breasts. Every thrust made her boobs bounce up toward her throat.

She squeezed him with her intimate muscles when he went to pull out, and his control snapped.

Yup. Ruined for all other men.

He unleashed the beast on her, pounding her pussy just like she needed. His prey, tied up and helpless, as he ravished her. She lay there at his mercy, taking everything he gave. And she loved it.

"Yes, yes, yes! Sam!"

White heat eclipsed her as her climax hit, her back arching. But he didn't slow down. Before she could come down from that orgasm, another built right on top of the first, and when he slipped a thumb over her clit, she detonated a third time. She managed to keep her eyes open, though, and saw the moment his climax hit. His mouth dropped open with a long moan as his hips stuttered. He threw his head back as his thrusts slowed, then stopped. Time stood still as neither of them moved from their positions while they caught their breath.

When he came back to Earth, Sam quickly unbound her hands, rubbing her wrists to get the blood flowing again. Then he grasped the condom and lifted off her, gently laying her stiff legs back down. He disappeared into the bathroom and returned with a warm washcloth and two water bottles. Sam cleaned between her legs with the washcloth, then threw it on the floor. Kneeling again, he carefully unbuckled her shoes, then gathered her in his arms and pulled her up to lay their heads on the pillow.

"I should shower," she croaked.

"In a bit," he said, handing her one of the waters. "Drink this first."

They both sat up and chugged. Before she knew it, half her bottle was gone.

"Wow. That was... holy shit." She looked over at his naked form in the bed next to her. Had that really happened?

He grinned. "That was just the beginning. I have plans for you, sweetness." Sam's mouth ghosted over her ear, and she shivered. "So many plans."

Frankie's nipples pebbled once more, and she took another swig of water. "I think I'm going to need this."

"Sweetheart, you have no idea."

FRANKIE HAD FALLEN INTO a deep sleep after round two, and a shower, which had nearly turned into round three. Something warm and slick lapping between her legs had her juices flowing again. What was up with her libido lately? After a dry spell that had lasted years, getting her good and sexed up apparently unleashed the flood waters.

A moan vibrating against her clit brought her fully awake.

Her eyes clenched shut as the orgasm washed over her, her hips thrusting into Sam's talented mouth. When she caught her breath and blinked them open, Sam laid next to her, his head propped on one hand, grinning down at her.

"Now that's the best part of waking up. Suck it, Maxwell House."

He laughed as he licked his lips. "That's Folgers."

"Whatever, hot stuff, you scrambled my brains."

"Good morning to you, too, sweetness."

"Mmph. Morning." She rubbed at her eyes as she sat up in bed. "Is there coffee in this room at all?"

"Yep. I'll get a pot started. Meanwhile, what do you want from room service? I'll order while you're in the bathroom."

"Whatever you're having."

He waggled his brows. "I already ate."

She playfully slapped him on the arm and slid past him off the bed. "Fine. I want pancakes."

"You got it." He lifted the receiver and spoke into the phone while Frankie disappeared into the bathroom.

After they both got dressed and devoured actual food, Frankie watched Sam flip the innocuous-looking business card around in his fingers.

"Is that the answer?"

"I guess." He stopped his movements and read it again. "It gives us coordinates and a date. But is that the date they arrive, or the date they leave?"

"It could be both." She sat up in her chair and took it from his hand. "We should check the coordinates back home, see if that gives us an address."

"You're right." He sighed. "It just seems more complicated than it needs to be."

Frankie chuckled. "Come on, you were expecting an engraved invitation? These guys aren't that classy."

He shrugged. "That's fair."

She rose from the table and started packing up her things, slipping the card into a secure pocket in her luggage. He stayed seated.

"In a hurry to get back to reality?"

She froze. While before she would have only heard the gruff tone, she'd been spending so much time around him, she could catch the mournful thread in Sam's voice. Instead of acting defensive, she turned to face him.

"Reality? What do you mean?"

He ran a hand through his hair and refused to meet her gaze. "I thought we could stay here a while. It's been like we're in our own little bubble... but you seem in a hurry to get away."

She shook her hair out, lifting the satin sleep bonnet and tucking it into her suitcase. "No, that's not... that's not it at all."

Frankie picked up her clothes strewn about the floor as she tried to explain. "I just want to get to the bottom of this so bad. I feel like we have the key in our hand. Once we figure out where those coordinates go, we should be that much closer to blowing this wide open."

Flustered, she balled the clothes from last night up and tossed them on the bed. "Were you going to pretend it didn't happen?"

"No!" He leaped from his seat and took her by the shoulders. "Last night was... it was..."

She smirked. Apparently, they were equally tongue-tied today. "It was for me, too," she assured him softly. Pressing her face into his chest, Frankie wrapped her arms around his waist. "But we have Sunday dinner with Mama Hunt tonight, and I want to deal with this clue before that."

"Good point. It wouldn't do to disappoint her." While Frankie didn't understand having a loving mother, she understood Roger's family was important to her friends.

What were she and Sam doing? Frankie had never had a reason to ask herself that before. Her feelings for Sam were unusual for her. She'd never let anyone get close enough for a serious relationship before. Her only sexual experiences had been one-time hookups, and a couple of friends with benefits situations. But he'd gotten under her skin and she wasn't sure what to do about it. It *felt* serious. Sam just gave off that vibe. For now, they were stuck together for as long as this project went on. She'd deal with it when he returned to Denver.

Yes, the question of what they were doing was definitely a Future Frankie problem.

Chapter 16

THE TRIP BACK TO Roger's house went too quickly. And unfortunately, Sam wasn't sure how to address the change in their dynamic.

He should really talk to Frankie, ask her if she wanted a relationship or not. Was she staying in Baltimore? Hell, he didn't even know if *he* was staying in Baltimore, although all signs pointed to yes. He'd take a pay cut to leave the FBI, but the lower stress, as well as getting to work with Roger again, was worth it.

And no more getting "borrowed" by other departments without his consent.

Jenna and Roger weren't home when they returned. Frankie grabbed her suitcase before he could. "You ready to figure out these coordinates?" She bounded up the stairs to the second floor, and he followed at a slower pace.

"You're like a dog with a bone," he said and chuckled. Her enthusiasm was adorable and infectious.

She poked her head out of her bedroom door with a cheeky grin. "I'm pretty sure you were the one with the bone."

He groaned at the terrible pun and went into his guest room. Then he had an idea.

Walking through their adjoining bathroom, he leaned against the doorway into her room. "You know, if you ever get sick of the air mattress, you're welcome to share with me."

Frankie eyed him from where she stood hanging her cocktail dress up in the closet. "You want to share a room and tell Roger and Jenna we're fucking?"

He shrugged, affecting a casual air he didn't feel in the least. "Would that bother you?"

She hummed, closing her suitcase into the closet. "I don't want them to think I'm taking advantage of you or something. After all, you're leaving at the end of the month."

Sam took a step into the room, feeling bold. "It's all but certain I'll be putting in my notice at the Bureau and coming right back to stay. There's nothing holding me to Denver now that my mom is in Florida." When she didn't say anything about him invading her space, he kept getting closer. "What are your plans after we finish this project?"

Frankie shrugged. "I don't have any. I have no home base, no clue what I'm going to do for work. All I can see are those victims. I don't even care what happens to me at the end of this."

"Really?" A tendril of black hair had fallen forward, and he reached out and tucked it behind her ear. If he'd thought she hadn't realized how close he was, he'd be wrong. She didn't even move her head. "There's nothing Frankie wants just for Frankie?"

She closed her eyes and tilted her head toward him. "I don't make plans, Sam. They've never done me any good. So I just take one day at a time." Opening her eyes, she gave him a sad, crooked smile. "No expectations, no pain."

He raised both eyebrows, but her mood turned on a dime as she pulled the card out of her pocket. "Let's find out where these coordinates lead." She grabbed him by the hand and led him to the room they were both using as an office.

Clearly, she didn't want to expand on her lack of foresight. That was okay; Sam could give her time. It seemed just as he solved one layer to the puzzle that was Frankie, another came along to stump him.

Mom always said he had the patience of Job.

When they got to their command central, Frankie shoved the card at him. "Let's go, soldier boy."

"Alright. Let me boot up Roger's desktop." He slid behind the desk and turned on the computer. Frankie appeared at his elbow, trying to squeeze her desk chair next to his. When it didn't fit, she left it at the end of the desk and sat anyway, craning her neck to see his screen.

It was a simple matter of entering the coordinates into Google Maps and seeing what came up. Not that there was much.

Frankie stood and leaned over his shoulder. "Where is it?"

"Let me get the satellite image." He clicked, and a building with a dock came into view. Zooming out, he realized it was close. Just outside Baltimore city limits, it was a free-standing house close to one of those newer housing developments. Ones where people paid top dollar for hastily built town homes that all looked exactly the same. And their backyards met the bay, so they had to cost a fortune.

But this house was older and removed from them. Far enough away to ensure privacy, but close enough to not raise suspicion. And it had a long dock slip out in the river, which fed into the Chesapeake Bay. Perfect for a larger boat to dock at unnoticed.

The date on the card was the end of the week.

"We need to talk to Roger and Jenna. Somehow, we have to get eyes on that place and see if they actually have the victims there, or if they're bringing them later."

Out of the corner of his eye, Sam saw Frankie's hand twitch. "Do you think they have security cameras?"

"I would assume so. They're probably tighter than Fort Knox, though. I doubt you can guess their password."

Frankie merely hummed but said nothing. "Where are Jenna and Roger, anyway?"

"I don't know." Sam didn't have to return his rental car just yet, but he hadn't planned to keep it for a second day. Once he got his life back in Denver packed up, he'd be driving his own car back to Baltimore.

He made a note of the address and saved photos of the area. Then he checked the time.

"I'm going to make a run to the grocery store for some wine, then I want to drop off the rental. I'll text Roger to meet me there."

"Sounds good."

Just as he picked up his phone, a video call came through. It was his mom.

"Guess that will have to wait," he said as he swiped the screen. "Hi, Mom."

"Sam! How is Baltimore?" Mom's face filled the screen, looking young despite the wrinkles. Florida agreed with her.

"It's great, Mom. How was your golf trip?"

"The trip was lovely, but the golf was terrible." She laughed at her usual joke. "What are you up to?"

Sam took a deep breath. He couldn't explain about their operation, but he could tell her a partial truth. "Just got back to Roger's after a work event last night. I had to go schmooze for him."

"Really? Did you have fun?"

He looked at Frankie out of the corner of his eye where she still stood, off to the side and out of the camera's view. "I didn't expect to, but I did." He pointed at the phone with a raised eyebrow, hoping she got the message he was trying to send. *Want to say hi?*

She crossed her arms and took a step backward. Giving her a small nod, he looked back at his mom. "What are you and Aunt June planning this week?"

"We have our book club on Wednesday, and then Friday, I think we're going on a whale watching cruise."

"Take pictures if you do."

"I will!" She adjusted her sunglasses, and he heard a sliding door open. "June! Sam's on the phone."

"Hi, Sam!" Aunt June peeked over Mom's shoulder. Her short gray hair tucked under a sunhat. "Nancy, I hate to tell you this, but we're going to be late for lunch."

"Oh dear, I forgot. Have a good time, Sam!"

"Thanks, Mom. You, too."

"Love you!"

"Love you, too, Mom." The screen went blank as she hung up.

"Your mom is cute. I can't believe how good she is with technology."

He chuckled. "Yeah, that's partly my fault. I was always obsessed with computers. And she was a teacher while I was growing up, so she ended up incorporating it into the classroom."

Furrowing his brow, Sam realized that Frankie never talked about her family. "Are you close with your parents?"

She snorted. "My mom is dead, and I don't know who my dad was. Could have been any of the guys she screwed to get drugs."

Well, shit, he really stepped in it. "I'm sorry."

"For what?"

"For bringing up a sore subject."

Frankie shrugged as she meandered over to the table where her laptop sat. "She overdosed when I was little. I don't remember much before I went into the foster system."

Sam dropped the subject with a nod. Suddenly, a lot of things about Frankie made sense.

"Weren't you going to text Roger?"

"Yeah, let me do that now." He picked his phone back up and started to type.

> **Sam: Hey we're back. I need to grab that wine for your parents and return my rental. Want to meet me there?**

> **Roger: Yeah, we shouldn't be long. Just finishing up lunch. See you in twenty?**

> **Sam: That works.**

He pocketed his phone and headed out the door. "You want to come to the grocery store with me?"

"Nah. I have some reading I want to do."

A cold weight settled in his gut. Sam couldn't shake the feeling he'd fucked up somehow. Backtracking, he pressed a quick kiss to her lips. "I'll be back with our friends."

She smiled, an honest one that reached her eyes. Thank goodness. "I'll be here." Relieved she wasn't upset about the mention of her past, he strolled away.

Chapter 17

MUCH LATER, FRANKIE AND Sam rode in the back of Roger's Chevy truck with the bottle of wine between them. They'd barely had time to fill Jenna and Roger in on what happened at the gala before it was time to leave for dinner. She glanced at Sam, then looked back out the window. He'd wanted her to meet his mom. Wasn't that moving a little fast? Just the thought made Frankie wipe her clammy hands on her jeans. They hadn't even told Jenna and Roger things had changed between them yet, for fuck's sake.

Frankie hadn't had any expectations pulling up to Roger's parents' house, but the two-story home with its wraparound porch painted a picture of an idyllic childhood. Roger had explained he was the oldest of four, with two brothers and a sister, who was the youngest. The party she'd crashed on her first day in Baltimore had been a sneaky set up by Roger so Nadia's boyfriend could pop the question.

Her experience growing up couldn't be any further from his.

She remembered bits and pieces of a small apartment, maybe a one-bedroom. Snatches of dirty walls and a persistent smell accompanied the always-present hunger whenever she remembered her birth mother. She'd become a ward of the state of Nevada at three, and then passed around various foster families. Many of their names had escaped her memories, but as she got older, they got clearer. The first Black family they'd placed her with moved out of state, so she ended up in a trailer park with a mixed family that yelled a lot. There was the family with the rottweiler who hated everyone. She'd gone to a lot more families than just the three, because she'd been a feral child and most people didn't want to put up with her.

Finally, as a teen, she'd ended up in a group home, with guardians who didn't care where they went as long as they didn't get caught skipping school. As far as meals were concerned, the children often fended for themselves. It was there on the family's untended computer she'd discovered a knack for hacking and started stealing identities. Eventually, she discovered cryptocurrency and how it could be modified. By the time she turned eighteen, she'd built a name for herself as a hacker you didn't want to deal with.

And now, at twenty-nine, she had no idea what to do with herself.

If Jenna was right, and the FBI was tracking her, then she didn't dare go back to her old way of life, whether the syndicate was looking for her or not. But what could she do? She had no other life skills.

Roger, Sam, and Jenna had all grown up with their parents. Jenna might not see eye to eye with hers, but at least she'd been *wanted*.

Frankie was still a bit in her head when Roger threw the truck in park. "We're here."

"Looks like Nadia drove tonight," Jenna commented on her view outside the window.

"How can you tell?" Frankie asked.

"She drives the ancient Chevy Prizm there. The one that looks like an antique?"

"Hey, that was my first car. It's not *that* old!" Roger scowled while Jenna's shoulders shook with suppressed laughter.

She turned around in the front seat to face Frankie. "The first time I was here, Finn said something about wanting a motorcycle, and their mother flipped. But Caleb had ridden over on his bike with Nadia on the back. It was awkward as *fuck*."

Frankie's eyes about popped out of her head. "So don't mention that I ride one, too. Got it."

Roger waved away her concern. "You're not her kid, so I don't think she'll say anything. But Jenna's right, Mom really stuck her foot in her mouth. I don't think she'll say anything about it again. Ever." With that, he opened the door and jogged around to Jenna's side. Frankie was so busy gawking at how cute and chivalrous he was that she didn't realize Sam had left the truck until her door opened as well.

"Oh! Um, thanks." Her cheeks heated as she slid from the seat and grasped his outstretched hand to hold on as she jumped from the running board. She looked up to see Jenna watching them closely. A raised eyebrow was all the communication she gave, but Frankie knew they were going to discuss this later.

Hoo boy.

Roger led them up the driveway to the front porch as a tall woman with a long reddish-brown braid, the same color as Roger's hair, swung the screen door open.

"Hello! Come on in! Dinner is almost ready." Her wide smile looked forced, and she spoke like a chihuahua on speed. Was she happy Frankie had tagged along? Or not?

"Hi, Mom." Roger leaned in for a hug, which she accepted, almost clinging to him for a minute.

Jenna hugged her as well, if only to save her boyfriend. "Hi, Judy."

"Hello again, Mrs. Hunt." Sam didn't have to bend far to hug the woman and hand her the wine.

"Sam, how thoughtful! Thank you, dear. And Frankie, thanks so much for coming." She even hugged Frankie, who stood there stiffly, then she disappeared into the kitchen, waving them into the living room as she did. Judy's energy was contagious, but it also seemed a touch manic. Frankie wasn't sure what to think.

They filed into the living room, where a couple sat on the couch. He had straight, black, chin-length hair, and an arm around a woman who had to be Roger's little sister. Caleb and Nadia.

"Hey, sis." Roger approached her and she stood to hug him.

"Hey, big bro." An understanding passed between brother and sister that Frankie could see but not understand.

"Has she been like this the whole time?" Roger pointed his thumb over his shoulder.

Nadia shrugged. "Pretty much, from what I can tell. She's not handling this well. It doesn't make sense. Y'all had countless deployments. Why this one?"

Caleb leaned forward with his elbows on his knees. "Maybe she just hid it better when y'all were younger?"

Nadia pushed her black plastic frames up her nose. "I don't know. All I know is she's fixated on my wedding and it's driving me crazy."

Roger patted her on the shoulder. "She needs a distraction."

Jenna slid in next to Roger. "What if you let her plan an engagement party for you? Would that get her off your back?"

Not really part of the conversation, Frankie turned to take in the Hunt's family home. Warm wood floors and plush furniture made for an inviting space. The dark green on the walls would make many homeowners pause, but it gave off such a cozy vibe. Photos of family vacations broke up the color. A bookcase filled with photo albums and souvenirs from faraway lands took up half the largest wall, and the brick fireplace in the corner looked like it came straight out of a Norman Rockwell painting.

"Jenna! Have you decided to run away with me yet?"

All eyes turned to look at the newcomer, who'd just left the powder room. Frankie looked back at Jenna just in time to see her friend's eyes roll.

"Frankie, Sam, this is Jon. He's Roger's younger brother. And a hopeless flirt." She glared at him. Roger's arms crossed over her chest while his face shot daggers at the grinning fool.

"I remember Sam. Roger introduced us over video chat after you graduated from Special Forces school."

"Ah yes, the squid." Sam reached over and shook his hand, while Frankie looked at them in confusion.

"He means I'm in the Navy." When she reached out to shake his hand, he instead brought her hand to his lips. "It's a pleasure, beautiful."

Sam gave a gratifying growl, and Jon backed away.

"Sam?"

"Later, Roger."

Frankie exchanged looks with Jenna, and they both had to stifle their laughter. Jon was good-looking, sure, but Frankie was already involved with her nerdy white boy.

An older man, probably Roger's dad, came to the doorway. "Come on into the dining room, everyone! Dinner's ready."

"Dad, you remember Sam? And this is Jenna's friend, Frankie."

"Nice to meet you, Frankie. I'm Irving Hunt." She shook the hand he held out.

"Thanks for inviting me."

"The more, the merrier! The boys always said Judy didn't know how to cook for less than a whole platoon." He chuckled as he led them to the back of the house, where a dining room with a long mahogany table and eight matching chairs stood ready to receive them, already bursting with side dishes.

"I had to feed four teenagers, you know."

Nadia snickered. "We weren't all teens at the same time, Mom."

"Well, it felt like the teen years went on forever." Judy said as she laid a platter of buttery breaded chicken on the tablecloth. "Darling, do you want to say grace?"

"Sure, love." Irving cleared his throat, and they all bowed their heads. "Dear God, we thank you for this food, and the friends and family you have brought to our table. We ask you to keep our Finley safe while he is overseas. In Your Name, Amen."

"Amen," they answered. Frankie sat next to Jenna, so she caught Nadia and Roger sharing a concerned look. She'd have to ask Roger about that later.

As the food came around and everyone dug in, the conversation turned to Nadia and Caleb's wedding. Poor

Nadia. She'd barely been engaged a week and her mother was asking for all sorts of details. Or rather, not asking, exactly.

"You should get married in June. It's such a good time of year."

"It's going to be so hot, Mom. I was thinking October."

Caleb tried to come to her aid. Bless the man. "And it gives us more time to plan."

"But you need to set a date so we can get the save the date cards sent, and the invitations, and your dress!"

Nadia cringed at the word "dress." "I told you we want to wait to set the date until we know Finn can be there. It's important."

"Of course you want Finn to be there. But his deployment is only for six months."

"But he's still stationed in Japan when he gets done there."

"And the Marines don't always stick to the plan, Mom. You know that." Judy bristled at Roger's gentle chiding.

"Well, this is as good a time as any to bring this up," Caleb said, throwing his napkin down.

"Did you decide?" Nadia asked him. He nodded.

The entire table's attention turned to him. Caleb swallowed and continued. "I've asked Jake, my best friend, to be my best man. But Nadia has four best friends, and I just have the one. I could ask their partners to stand with me, but I suspect we're going to be doing this a lot over the next several years, so there will be other chances for them. But it would mean a lot to me, and I think to Nad as well…" He looked over at her and she nodded, her eyes watering, "If Roger, Jon, and Finn would stand with me as groomsmen."

Roger didn't say anything, just pushed his chair back with a sniff, and waved for Caleb to get up. They met in the middle of the doorway and hugged behind Judith, who bawled into her napkin. Frankie couldn't hear what they said to each other, but Roger's eyes were wet when he pulled back, nodding. Jon stood and clapped Caleb on the back, also murmuring an agreement, and then they returned to their seats. Frankie looked across the table at Sam, who was grinning at Roger like he couldn't be happier for his best friend.

Frankie had never been to a wedding, but she knew that usually the groom picked his friends or family to stand with him. The impact of asking Nadia's brothers instead didn't escape her. Not completely anyway.

Once the rest of the table had dried their eyes and resumed dinner, Mrs. Hunt seemed placated. Frankie's mind wandered to her own mother. If her life had been different, would she have had to deal with wedding drama, too? Provided she ever actually *got* married.

She shook the idea away. She'd never believed in what-ifs and should-have-beens. They'd never done her any good. She described her life motto as, "It is what it is." Frankie had no one. And it didn't really matter to her she didn't.

Well, maybe she had Jenna. But she'd had other friends in the past that faded away. Frankie had built her life on being independent and not needing anyone else. It was better not to get attached than to be disappointed all the time.

Her life as a foster kid hadn't been kind. She'd hated having to move around so much. The constant uprooting of her life brought a myriad of challenges and difficulties. Each time she settled into a new place, it felt like starting from scratch all over again. The instability took a toll on her education as well, as she had to adjust to new schools and curricula frequently. Making friends became a daunting task, knowing that she would eventually have to say goodbye and leave them behind. When she'd been at a school and ended up being removed from the home she lived in, she would lose any friends she made just as quickly. She'd learned early on not to get close to people. It wasn't worth the effort, or the heartache, every time she had to leave. Far easier in the long run to stay aloof and separate.

She glanced up at Sam again, then back at her plate. It might be nice to have someone to come home to. Someone to watch a movie with or play a video game. Sam was a type of steady that intrigued her.

Frankie had never considered any of that domestic shit before. Was that something she could have?

Chapter 18

IT WAS LATE WHEN they got home, and by some unspoken agreement, they all headed upstairs to get ready for bed. He'd just taken his shirt off when he heard Frankie's voice in his room.

"Is it just me, or is Roger's family like the fuckin' Brady Bunch?"

Sam smirked and turned around, watching her appreciate the view as he answered. "Wasn't the Brady Bunch a blended family? Roger and his siblings all have the same parents."

"Ugh, whatever. You know what I mean, right?"

He nodded as she came closer, and his brain registered she wore only a long t-shirt and nothing else. Then his cock registered it.

She reached out and palmed his erection through his pants. "Someone's happy to see me."

"Sitting across from you was torture tonight."

"Well, what are you up to now?"

"I was going to shower. Care to join me?"

She hummed and stroked him through the cloth. "I'd love to."

Turning, she led him back to the bathroom, pulling her shirt off as they went. Then he got a view of her naked backside, proving she wasn't wearing anything under it. Reaching out, Sam clutched at her plump ass cheeks, then spanked one side. She squealed in surprise.

"Naughty girl, no panties."

She turned her head and winked. "Easy access, silly. Now let's get in this shower so I can get you clean."

"After you dirty me up, you mean."

Frankie threw her head back and laughed. "Of course."

He heated the water while she tucked her hair under a shower cap. Then her hands were back on him, pulling his jeans and boxer briefs down over his ass. Teeth nipped at his glutes, causing him to yelp and straighten up.

"Tease." He grabbed for her as she tried to dance out of his grasp, but the small bathroom didn't give her anywhere to run. Sam kicked the last of his clothes off and pulled her into his arms. He laid a kiss on her plush lips, and she opened for him on a sigh, her tongue sliding out to dance with his. Then he pinched her nipple.

"Ooh!" She jumped, and he had to tilt his head back to avoid her head breaking his nose. He grinned at her pouting lip.

"Payback." Then he bent to kiss the tip of her breast and soothe the ache. She groaned and pressed her hands to the back of his head, whining when he pulled away. "Come on, sweetness. Shower time."

"Fine." They stepped into the bathtub, the shower head raining hot water down. While they'd played around, the shower had filled with steam, fogging the glass and making it feel like their own little world. Facing her toward the water, Sam pulled Frankie's back against his front and slid his hands over her wet, lush curves.

She laid her head back against his shoulder, his pale fingers glowing against her dark, smooth skin. His cock stood at attention, digging into the round globes in front of him. He bent down and his lips found her ear, her neck, and one hand cupped a breast, while the other reached down to strum her clit.

His sweetness trembled in his arms as he drove her closer and closer to her peak.

"Don't stop, don't stop, oh my God, Sam! SA—" He pinched her nipple and then pressed his hand over her mouth before she could scream.

"We have to be quiet, unless you *want* Roger and Jenna to hear us."

She shook her head, patting the hand over her mouth with hers, then pressing his other hand back onto her clit. He hadn't realized he'd left her hanging. Sam redoubled his efforts on her sweet spot, rolling it under his thumb as two fingers slid inside her hot little channel, stroking in a "come-hither" motion.

It didn't take long before Frankie's eyes were rolling back in her head, her whole body shaking with her orgasm. Sam pressed firmly on the little spongy bit of tissue inside her and her clit at the same time, drawing her orgasm out. "That's it, sweetness. Give it to me." When she went lax in his arms, he took his hands away and used them to hold her up instead.

"Damn," she gasped. Before he could reach for the body wash, she turned around. "Hold on, soldier boy. Your turn."

Sam shook his head, but she pushed him into the spray of the water and back against the cool tile. Her hands caressed down his chest and stomach, followed by her little pink tongue. When he realized she was going to her knees, he cupped her chin.

"Don't finish me off, sweetness. I want to come in that pussy." Then he swore. "I left the condoms in the bedroom."

She shrugged. "I have an implant. And I'm clean."

He groaned and released her. "Just had my physical before I came down here and I'm clean, too." His hands clenched as she licked a line up the underside of his cock, and her hands gently squeezed his balls.

"Let's make a game of it." She grinned up at him, her eyes full of mischief. "Can you see the clock from here?"

Sam wiped some of the fog away from the glass. "Yeah."

"If I can't make you blow in a minute, then I'll stop, and you can fuck me bare."

"I love a game with no losers." He waited until the second hand crossed the six. "Go."

WHILE SHE AGREED WITH Sam that there would be no losers here, Frankie had every intention of losing this game. As hard as he'd made her come a few minutes ago, she desperately wanted to fuck him in the shower the minute he said something. But she also wanted his cock in her mouth, something more for him than her.

Running her tongue around the head, she sucked the crown into her mouth. Then she stared up at him, watching his face as she flicked her tongue against his frenulum. He shuddered and closed his eyes, dropping his jaw on a silent moan.

"Watch the clock, baby," she reminded him, then slid her mouth over his dick, bringing it all the way to the back of her throat. She gave it everything she had for the rest of her minute, hollowing her cheeks and repeatedly bringing him back to her throat and swallowing. His thighs trembled beneath her hands and she knew he was close.

Then his hands were under her arms, and he lifted her to her feet. "Minute's up," he panted. "Put your hands on the wall, sweetness. I can't be gentle."

"Fuck, yes." She spun and put her hands on the tiled wall, bending over to give him access. His hands traced reverently over her ass, then spanked her right cheek lightly.

"God*damn*, I love this ass. It's perfection."

Smirking, Frankie waved it at him. "Get in me, soldier boy."

"I need a minute or this isn't going to take long." He took a few deep breaths, then he grasped her hips. His cock lined up at her entrance, and Frankie quivered in anticipation.

When he slammed into her, hitting her g-spot so perfectly, her orgasm started building. He took her hard and fast, hitting that spot every single time. Then his hand dropped down to rub on her clit again, and the pleasure in her core spun tighter and tighter.

Frankie muffled her moans in her arm as he hammered her into the wall, moaning her name. It had never sounded sweeter.

"God, Francesca... Come for me, Francesca. Come!"

That did it. Her orgasm swept through her, a tornado of white-hot pleasure that left her boneless and panting. His hips faltered in their rhythm, then he shot inside her, warm liquid splashing inside her walls. Sam pulled her to standing and turned her around, wrapping his arms around her as they came down from the high.

Frankie didn't remember any of her previous partners wanting to cuddle so much. She'd never had anyone cuddle her before. Maybe her mother, when she was little and her mother had a sober day. But no one since.

She liked it.

They washed each other as the water turned cold, hopping out of the shower with a laugh at themselves. After a quick towel-dry, Sam took her by the hand and led her back into his room.

"You were serious about sharing, huh?"

He nodded, a pink blush staining his cheeks. "If you don't want to, that's fine."

She held onto his hand and thought for a moment. Staying the whole night was tempting, but she worried about what would happen if she got too attached.

Hell, she might already *be* too attached. It wasn't like she had any experience to say if she was or not.

But Frankie was all about taking it one day at a time, and this felt like a new experience she needed to try. "Let me grab my sleep bonnet from my room, then I'll be back."

He leaned over and kissed her. "You don't have to wear anything, you know."

She grinned and hopped out of his arms. "If I don't wear the bonnet, my hair will be unbearable. But I can sleep naked otherwise." She jogged across the bathroom and grabbed her bonnet from her makeshift nightstand next to the air mattress. Tucking her hair into it as she walked back, she put some sway in her hips when she saw Sam watching her from the doorway.

He groaned. "I need some recovery time before I go again, sweetness."

She winked. "I know. Feel free to wake me up any way you want, hot stuff."

They slipped between the cool sheets together, and Frankie turned on her side to sleep. Sam curled behind her, one arm banded around her middle.

She drifted off into a deep slumber, contentment filling her veins for the first time in a long while.

GENTLE STROKES ON HER breast and a mouth sucking on her neck slowly brought Frankie's conscious mind back to the surface. She lay there in a half-dream, half-waking state as something hard and long slipped between her thighs and massaged along her wet slit, rubbing her clit on every pass. Shuddering in Sam's arms, she opened her eyes to a dimly lit room. Early morning light peeked around the blackout curtains on the windows, so she knew it was morning.

And what a morning it was.

She hummed low in her throat, and her voice rasped from sleep. "A girl could get used to this."

Sam's chuckle in her ear only made her wetter. "Good morning, Francesca."

"Good morning, indeed." He slipped inside her and made soft, sweet love to her, both of them moaning as they came to completion.

Holy shit. He was smart, knew his way around computers, and he danced with her. How could she give this man up?

A rapping at the door jolted her out of her afterglow. "Hey, when you guys are done in there, Roger's making breakfast. Then he wants to go over our game plan for Thursday night."

Cold shock made Frankie freeze in Sam's bed. Jenna knew!

Sam held a finger to her lips. "I'll be down."

Jenna chuckled. "I've already been to Frankie's room, Sam. I know she's in there with you."

Frankie swore under her breath, then climbed out of his bed.

"Did you check the bathroom?" Sam called out.

"Well, the door to the bathroom is wide open, and she wasn't in there when I checked thirty seconds ago."

Sam covered his mouth, suppressing laughter. Frankie had to stifle giggles, too. This was fun.

"Maybe she went for a walk?"

Something smacked against the door. Jenna's head, based on the groan of frustration she let out. "Look, it's pretty obvious after last night that you're fucking, and I don't care. I just want my scrambled eggs. And I would like to know what the plan for Thursday is."

"Alright, Jenna, we'll be right down." Sam looked back at Frankie and shrugged, his chest vibrating with glee. As soon as Jenna walked away, they fell to the bed, holding their sides and trying not to make too much noise.

"Let me go pee, then we can both brush our teeth." Frankie rose once more and actually made it into the bathroom this time, shutting both doors.

She'd have to wake up really early in the morning to get one over on the Sly Fox.

Chapter 19

DESCENDING THE STAIRS TOGETHER, Sam's cheeks heated when he saw Jenna smirking at him over her coffee mug. "Good morning."

"Morning," he said, wary of the sly redhead.

Meanwhile, Frankie pranced over like this was any other Monday.

"Morning, babes. Mm, that smells good, Roger."

Roger stood at the stove, a skillet of liquid gold on the burner. "Should be ready soon."

"Coffee?" Sam asked with a nod in Frankie's direction.

"Yes, please." She slid into a seat next to Jenna.

He pulled down a mug, aware of the two pairs of eyes boring into him. "How do you take it?"

"Any way I find it, big boy." At the confusion on his face when he turned around, she laughed. "Sorry, old joke. Splash of creamer and two sugars, please. Or milk, or whatever is around."

"You got it." Roger reached into the refrigerator on his other side and handed the milk to Sam. He prepared her coffee the way she'd described, then slid the mug across the island to her.

She took a sip and hummed. "Perfect."

He turned back to hide the smile on his lips and poured his own cup. An elbow to his shoulder made him turn toward the stove.

Roger had a questioning look on his face. Even after all their time apart, they could still communicate without saying a word. The way he angled his head, with that particular expression, was his way of asking if Sam had slept with Frankie. Sam answered with a slightly smug grin and a lift of his chin.

His friend's reaction was both surprised and proud. Yeah, Sam's old problems of putting his foot in his mouth seemed to disappear on that dance floor at the gala. Maybe that had been his problem all those years. Either he just needed something else for his feet to do, or Mom had been right all along and dancing was the way to a girl's heart.

He'd have to tell her the next time he saw her.

Roger laid four plates of scrambled eggs on the island along with a plate of bacon, and for several minutes, the only sounds in the kitchen were the sounds of appreciation for the food. Once their stomachs were full, Jenna got up to brew another pot of coffee and Roger cleared his throat.

"Well, I see you didn't tell us *every*thing that happened at the gala."

Frankie stuck her tongue out at Roger. "Mind ya business."

"You misunderstand, Frankie. I'm thrilled." Roger chuckled into his mug.

"We were more focused on catching you up on the information we got. It was more imperative than what happened between us personally." Sam gave Roger the hairy eyeball that would tell him not to piss his girl off.

Roger pointed a finger in the air. "That reminds me. I think we need information on that warehouse before we decide anything about Thursday night."

"Agreed." Sam said, and the girls nodded. "Let's start with the legal stuff. We should find out who owns it, for starters."

"It's probably a shell company that's run by the syndicate." Frankie drained her mug and set it down on the counter. "I want to know how secure it is."

Jenna propped her head up with her hand. "It feels too easy to me. He just gave you a date. Are we sure that's the right one?"

"That's why we're moving in early, to try to get our evidence before they move them," Sam reminded her. Jenna and Roger shared a look that he wasn't sure how to interpret.

"I'll get started as soon as we're done." He decided to forget the second cup of coffee and rinsed his mug out before putting it in the top of the dishwasher.

Roger huffed in annoyance. "Alright, then we're going fishing this afternoon."

"Since when have you known me to go fishing?"

"You're on vacation!"

Jenna playfully shoved Roger in the shoulder. "We should all go sightseeing. I still haven't got to play tourist in this town."

Frankie shrugged. "I'm game. I want to do some digging of my own, though."

"Alright, I got some admin stuff to do. Let's work until lunch, then we'll go out and play tourist."

Jenna clapped her hands in glee. "This is going to be fun!"

Sam just shook his head and returned to the stairs. Frankie wasn't far behind.

"Hey, Sam, do you think one of those coded addresses is the same as the one Neil gave us?"

Sam stopped at the top of the staircase and turned, and Frankie nearly fell backward. He grabbed at her shoulder to steady her. "Frankie, you're a genius! I bet that will break the code wide open!" He bent to kiss her, but she put a hand against his mouth to stop him.

"Not on the stairs, soldier boy. I don't want to brain my damage."

He couldn't help but grin at the silly saying, grabbing her hand and hauling her up after him. Once safely in the hall, he picked her up and kissed her soundly on the mouth.

She patted his chest as he set her back down. "Don't distract me, babe. We have work to do."

"Yes, ma'am." He followed her into the office, and they got to work.

About four hours later, Sam and Frankie stretched at nearly the same time. "Were you able to break it?"

She groaned. "I cataloged every address and analyzed the character structure, and I have it narrowed down to a few.

I wish I had some kind of program that could just find the likeliest match."

"Sorry, sweetness. We'll just have to do it the old-fashioned way."

"Yeah, I know. I'll get back to it later. I want to assess the security of the address we *do* have."

"Let's go down and see where Roger wants to play tourist."

Frankie chuckled. "Hopefully, we're stopping for lunch first."

Roger's idea of playing tourist consisted of taking his girl and their friends to the Inner Harbor. The weather had turned chilly, especially with the wind off the bay, so the girls talked Roger out of a water taxi ride. Instead, they drove as far as they could and parked in a public garage, then walked to Harborplace. Inside the mall-like building, Roger pointed out a lobster roll shop. "I haven't had one of these in ages."

It smelled like fried butter and happiness. Sam's stomach wasn't the only one growling. He and Frankie each got a classic. She got the potato salad while he had the coleslaw. After that, they took their drinks and walked along the brick promenade.

Frankie pointed out a sign. "Jenna, when this is over, I'm taking a day and going there."

The sign was for the Museum of Maryland African American History and Culture, talking about a special Frederick Douglass exhibit. Sam filed that away for future date possibilities.

"That looks cool," Jenna replied. "I want to go to the aquarium."

"We can do both!"

"Are we invited on this day trip?" Roger asked, pulling Jenna under his arm.

"I don't know. Maybe it's just a girls' trip."

Sam slipped an arm around Frankie's shoulders, amazed when she didn't pull away. He didn't have to be jealous of Roger now that he had Frankie.

Now if he could just convince her to stay in Baltimore when he returned.

His resignation letter sat in a folder on his desktop back home. He'd print and deliver it in person when he got back to Denver, and then move out here. He couldn't wait.

Between having his friends close and his girl, the captivating city was just the Old Bay on the crab cake.

AFTER THEIR OUTING, WHICH was punctuated by even more great seafood, Frankie slid into her office chair despite the late hour. She had a building to assess.

While Sam had discovered the legal hoops that the syndicate had gone through in order to own the building without it being obvious, Frankie was more concerned with how they were going to get in.

Because make no mistake, Foxy was going in.

While Sam was under the impression they were just gathering photos and such that hadn't been stolen from the servers, Jenna and Roger were hoping to get evidence of a different nature. The human one.

They'd get the other evidence as well, because the victims might not want to testify.

Roger had promised he'd tell Sam closer to Thursday, the day before the auction they were told about was to take place.

So Frankie did what she had always done. It was easy to get specs on the syndicate buildings, because they had them all recorded. In fact, Frankie decided it would be best to hack their cameras early, to be sure she could do so on D-day.

She didn't hear Sam come up behind her as she executed the skills she'd used for so long. When he spoke, she was busy looking around the house by way of the cameras the syndicate had placed around.

"What is that?"

Frankie jumped in her seat and yelped. Turning, she laid a hand over her pounding heart. "Oh, my God! You scared the hell outta me!" Sam leaned back over her chair, having dodged her skull to avoid a broken nose. "It appears to be a bathroom." Gross. Wasn't that extra illegal or something? They weren't taking any chances with the people they would keep here.

Unfortunately for her, the house was completely deserted. It would have been nice to have confirmation this was being used, and not a decoy.

"How did you get in there?"

She rolled her eyes. "Through a terminal, how else? They had the specs listed in the database, like always."

"I see," he said as he pushed his glasses up his nose. "So it's empty?"

"For now." She flipped through a few more cameras, landing on the one in the kitchen. "There's fruit in that bowl there, and no flies, so I'm assuming someone's gone on a grocery run to prepare for the auction."

"You're right. I was worried it was a false lead, but I'm thinking it's not."

Frankie beamed. "Now, if I can just crack the other addresses, we'd be in business."

"We need more evidence than stolen invoices, but you're on the right track." He watched her verify the building was empty, then closed her software down. There was nothing more she could do tonight. They just had to wait for Thursday.

Once the screen went dark, Frankie realized how weary her eyes were. "I'm going to shower and go to bed," she announced, rising from her chair. She nudged him with her hip, his eyes still on her monitor. "You coming?"

"Yeah, I'll jump in the shower after you." Sam seemed distracted. Frankie furrowed her brow in confusion.

"Alright."

As she got ready for the shower, she wondered what could be wrong with Sam. Then again, they'd had a very long day. Most likely, he was just tired. She had already decided she wasn't up to any fun activity tonight, anyway.

That was probably all it was.

Chapter 20

SAM FROWNED AT THE black screen on Frankie's makeshift desk. His thoughts had scrambled as he'd watched her work. He rubbed at his eyes, but he couldn't erase what he'd seen. *I just can't believe it.*

He had his work phone in his hand before he realized he'd even left the office. The sound of the shower running reminded him Frankie was next door, wet and naked. But for once, his cock wasn't interested. He was far more concerned by what he'd seen on the screen. Awareness of her proximity made him get up off his ass and head back to the office for some privacy.

Shaking his head, Sam paced as he tried to talk himself out of what he knew he had to do. His mouth had dried out like he'd been arguing, but he had barely said a word since he'd seen it. Seen her work.

What were the chances that he'd find the Sly Fox's hacker in his best friend's home?

Ridiculous, he told himself. *That's like stumbling onto winning lottery numbers. It's been so long since you looked at the files that you're misremembering the hacker's signature.*

Unfortunately, there was only one way to find out for sure.

Using his phone, he brought up his remote desktop from back home. The files for Roger's security camera breach were still on his hard drive, and it didn't take long for him to pull up the file.

His fingers trembled as he tried to open the file on the touch screen of his phone, suddenly too cold for the body heat to register. He pressed harder, finally getting the button to function.

What would he say to her if it were true? Closing his eyes, Sam prayed he didn't have to figure it out. If — no, *when* the signatures didn't match, she wouldn't even know he'd ever suspected her.

It took time for the files to load over the remote access app. But he didn't want to wait to upload the software onto Roger's computer. Especially without permission. And if he asked permission, he'd have to tell Roger why.

Finally, his personal desktop appeared on the much smaller screen of his phone. He shook as he navigated to the folder he wanted. A sour taste rose in the back of his throat, but he kept going, opening the file in question. When he'd reviewed his notes from Roger's security breach, Sam slapped a hand over his mouth. His chest tingled, and his head swam. Forcing himself to take a deep breath, Sam read the notes again and again. Swaying on his feet, he collapsed into his chair. But there was no denying it anymore.

The woman he'd been helping, the sassy sweetness he'd been inside and had been falling for, was the hacker.

God, he needed a beer.

FRANKIE FINISHED HER SHOWER, dressing in her pajamas in her own room. She wondered if Sam was feeling sick, the way he'd shut down in the office earlier. Peeking her head inside his room, she found it empty. That seemed odd.

She padded down the hall barefoot, surprised to find the office light on, but still no Sam. Well, she wasn't tired anymore. She sat down at her computer, firing it back up and cracking her knuckles while she waited. Time to see what she could find about these addresses. Once they had proof that the victims were being shipped between states, the FBI would have more cause to search.

Her software kicked in the same as it always did. She'd spent so much time in the syndicate's servers through her remote access point that it came up automatically, along with the IP scrambler. That's when she noticed the new file.

Now, Frankie had been over every inch of this server, and while new files appeared in the sub-folders on a somewhat regular basis, this one had appeared in the main folder. Just sitting out there waiting for her to discover it. The other weird thing was, every other file on the server was a PDF or a JPG. But this was an MP4.

Could she have stumbled on a recording of the syndicate's heinous crimes?

She bit her lip, considering whether she had the stomach to view it or not. If it gave her nightmares, she'd have a sexy as hell teddy bear to make her feel better. But it could give them the edge with the government and make them take this seriously.

Sam had told her nothing they found through hacking would be admissible in court, but with enough proof, the FBI could get a warrant to search the server themselves.

That settled her mind.

Carefully, she copied the file to her own computer, and then opened it in her media player. The video opened with no sound, and instead of the horrific scene Frankie had braced herself against, she saw something far more sinister.

Photos of her and Sam in the hotel room. It was like a voyeuristic slideshow of their first night together.

Sam kissing her against the door. Ripping each other's clothes off over several pictures. Then the two of them on the bed, him worshipping her curves as her back arched.

She watched it all the way through before the words on the screen registered in her shock-addled brain. *TRAITOR* flashed in red at the top of the images. Along the bottom of the screen, the words "Does the Fed know who he took to his bed?" scrolled by, over and over.

Hypnotized with horror, Frankie wasn't sure how many times she watched the erotic flipbook of their night after the gala before she finally shut her connection to the servers and stopped the video. She nearly put it in the recycling bin but hesitated. There might be some way to track who had outed them with it.

But it didn't take a genius to figure it out. Neil, or whatever his real name was, had clocked them immediately. All the more reason to suspect the information he gave them was false.

And now she didn't dare hack into the security cameras again. Not from her computer, anyway.

"We're fucked."

She had to find the others.

SAM SHUFFLED DOWN TO the kitchen and grabbed a beer from the fridge. Popping the cap, he drank it down swiftly, then grabbed a second as soon as the first was empty. He swiped a hand through his hair as he drank the next one slower.

God, was he trying to get drunk? He was too old for that shit anymore. No, he knew all he wanted was to numb the pain. There had to be a logical explanation for why Frankie and the Sly Fox's hacker had the same signature.

Duh, because they're the same person, moron.

He drank a bit faster to shut up that annoying internal voice.

A reddish glow in the dark backyard drew his eyes to the screen door. Something pulled him out toward it, some siren song his ears couldn't make out.

Sitting in camping chairs next to a dying fire in the pit were Jenna and Roger. He had her tucked under his arm as they watched the flames dance, bundled up in hoodies to ward off the night chill.

Roger raised a hand in greeting, and Jenna lifted her head off his chest. "Hey, Sam. What's up?"

A strange thought occurred to him. When he'd been a kid watching his mom crochet, he often helped by rolling yarn into a ball from the skein for her. Many times, he'd pull and pull on an end, only to yank out a giant mess of tangled yarn. His mother had laughed and explained that her knitting and crochet friends referred to that as "yarn barf." It would take them ages to unwind and detangle. His brain felt like that yarn barf.

He stared at Roger, willing him to make sense of the knotted mess that was his mind. "I... I need to talk to you," he finally muttered.

Jenna patted Roger on the knee and stood up. "Here, take my seat. I'm getting too cold, anyway." She bent over and gave Roger a quick peck. "I'll see you inside."

He nodded and gestured for Sam to sit down. Sam sat on the edge of the chair, leaning forward on his knees. Once the backdoor had shut, he turned to Roger.

"Frankie hacked into the security cameras for that address. It's empty for now, but we don't think for long."

Roger nodded, as if this made perfect sense. "They probably don't keep them in any one place for too long. It'd be too dangerous."

Sam licked his lips as he realized Roger wasn't surprised at all. He'd... *expected* Frankie to hack the cameras.

"There's something else you should know." He watched Roger's face in the dying firelight. "Frankie's hacker signature matches the one that hacked your security cameras." Roger winced. Sam's body tensed and flushed with heat that had nothing to do with the beer. "You *knew*?" He chugged his beer while Roger scrubbed a hand over his face.

"Look, I'm sorry you found out this way... I wanted to tell you, but I had to protect Jenna."

"What does Jenna have to do with any of this? Frankie's the reason those creeps got into her apartment! How are they even friends?"

Roger grimaced. "It's... it's complicated."

Sam's voice started to rise. "Well, un-complicate it. What the actual fuck is going *on*, Roger?"

Roger raised his hands in a defensive posture. "Frankie was given incorrect information, and that's why she hacked into my cameras. She and Jenna used to work together before Jenna left the organization."

"Left the organi... wait, you mean the *syndicate*? Who we know is trafficking humans?"

His former friend sighed. "They weren't involved in that, which should be obvious. Since Frankie arrived, she's been obsessed about taking them down."

Sam pinched the bridge of his nose, pulling slow and steady breaths to try to keep himself calm. "So then, what were they involved with, exactly?"

"Frankie was a hacker for them."

"Frankie was the hacker working with the Sly Fox, that the FBI was hunting!"

The look of pain on Roger's face took time to register in his brain. "Wait... are you saying... what I *think* you're saying?"

Roger couldn't look him in the eye. Sam thought about Frankie's nickname for Jenna. Foxy. Sly Fox.

Jesus, Mary, Joseph, and all the disciples, as his mother would say.

Sam's jaw clenched. "Your girl is the Sly Fox, isn't she, Roger?"

Roger let out a slow breath, then finally turned his head to face Sam. Regret and relief were written all over his face. Maybe later Sam could contemplate how hard it had been to keep that secret from someone he called a brother. After, he got over the betrayal.

"I'm sorry, Sam." Roger's Adam's apple bobbed as he gulped. "She was out of that life and by the time I knew about it..."

"You were already sleeping with her." Sam deadpanned. He closed his eyes, unable to look at Roger cringe. A man he'd trusted with his life, a man he clearly didn't know as well as he thought.

"She isn't that person anymore, Sam, and she hadn't been for a while when we met."

It was all too much to take in. Sam looked at the inch of beer in his bottle, and the fire that was nearly out. He rose and poured the last of his drink on the fire, smothering the embers.

And it had been such a great day, too.

"I'll find a hotel tomorrow."

"Sam, please, I'm sorry I didn't tell you."

"You don't think it would have been important for me to know that I've been staying under the same roof as wanted criminals? Criminals I was fucking tasked with locating?" He scoffed. "Some friend you turned out to be."

Roger gripped his hair in his fists. "I couldn't let you turn her in!"

"Because you wanted to fuck her!"

"No, because I love her!" Roger shouted back. "And this syndicate prays on the lonely, the strays. She might have had a family, but they weren't talking to her... and then the syndicate got their claws in her."

"And they *forced* her to steal?" Sarcasm dripped from his lips.

"They're insidious." He startled as Jenna reappeared, the clouds in the night sky giving her the opportunity to sneak up on him.

"They ply you with food and a roof over your head and ask for small favors at first. But then they ask for bigger and bigger favors and before you know you it, you're on a heist with other members. By the time you realize who these people really are, they'll kill you if you try to leave. The only reason I managed to disappear for as long as I did was because of careful planning. And the only reason I'm still alive is because of Frankie erasing us from the database."

He stared at the short redhead before him. Calm radiated from her while he battled a storm inside.

Frankie's worried voice from the back porch broke their standoff in the dark. "Um, guys? We have a bigger problem right now."

Jenna turned around to face her friend. "What's that?"

Yes, what could possibly be bigger than the betrayal from his best friend and the girl he'd been falling for?

Frankie's silhouette stood out against the light coming from the kitchen. "We've been made."

Chapter 21

Nausea clawed at the back of Frankie's throat as she paced between the living room and the back door in the kitchen, chewing on her nails. Sam, Jenna, and Roger trailed in, but she didn't look up. She couldn't deal with the anger and judgment in Sam's eyes right now. Jenna approached her like a skittish wild animal.

"Frankie, what do you mean, 'We've been made'?"

Frankie looked up at her only friend and focused on Jenna's face as she spoke. "There was a video on the server tonight. They added it in the last hour since I accessed the cameras in the... house." Such a benign term didn't accurately describe the evil that had happened there, but it was all she had. "I thought maybe it would be video proof that we could use, but when I opened it, it was pictures of... of Sam and me." Her cheeks heated, and she cast her gaze downward. "They must have used a drone to get up to the window of the hotel room. And the words on the screen called Sam out for being a Fed." At his sharp intake of breath, Frankie looked up at him even as the pinprick of tears threatened to consume her. "I... I don't know what to do."

Roger and Sam swore in unison as Jenna wrapped her arms around Frankie in a hug. "I'm sorry, Frankie."

Frankie held onto her, grateful for this anchor in the storm raging in her heart. The sheer violation of someone else looking into their room, and taking photos... She didn't realize she was sobbing or hyperventilating until Roger held a paper bag to her lips and walked her through deep breaths.

Jenna had released her and now rubbed her back. Frankie leaned on her sideways as her breathing calmed down.

She stole a glance at Sam. He'd crossed his arms over his chest, standing back from everyone else. The clenched jaw and glare he was sending their way made it clear where he stood.

It looked like their fling had come to a premature end.

Jenna led her over to the couch, and Frankie sat down, hugging her knees to her chest. Roger came to stand with them, but Sam still hung back.

"It's late, girls. There's nothing we can do tonight. My security system will alert us if anything crosses my property line. Let's get some sleep, and then we'll reevaluate in the morning." He turned to face Frankie. "I'm sure you'll want to get back on the server long enough to erase that video. I'm hoping it's the only file, but I doubt it."

She scrubbed a hand over her eyes. What a mess. "Yeah, I'll do that."

Roger gave her a tight smile, his fatigue obvious. "We'll figure it out tomorrow. You're not alone, Frankie."

Frankie didn't think she could sleep, but Roger had made his point. Jenna slowly rose and seemed reluctant to leave her.

"Go ahead, I'm not far behind." Her only friend in the world squeezed her shoulder and followed Roger up the stairs. Sam watched them go with an icy stare, his hands clenched when his arms dropped.

He'd figured out who she was. And that had told him who Jenna was.

Damn it, she really shouldn't have fallen... into bed with him. She knew it would spell trouble. But she just couldn't help herself, could she?

"Are you done with your pity party?" Sam finally addressed her.

Her mouth dropped open at the audacity of this guy. Anger burned away her guilt. "There are two people in those photos, you know. I doubt you want your boss at the FBI to see photos of you banging me."

He tilted his head at her. "Blackmail? Really?"

"I'm just saying they know who you work for. It's very possible they're going to make contact to buy your silence."

Sam scoffed. "You realize the FBI is already gunning for them for the jewel thefts, right? Finding out they deal in human trafficking too is just another nail in the coffin."

Frankie rubbed the back of her neck. "Larry said they have agents on the payroll, so the whole thing might get swept under the rug. That's why I came here asking for help. I can't let them get away with trafficking innocent people."

"Sounds to me like you're just trying to use them to kill your guilt."

"It's called redemption, asshole!" Her volume had gotten away from her, but the click of the hall light upstairs turning off reminded her that Jenna and Roger were trying to sleep.

"Just go to bed. Maybe you'll dream about empathy." Frankie stalked away and strode up the stairs, navigating her way easily to her room. She threw herself onto the air mattress and immediately missed the actual mattress in Sam's room. Safe and alone, she curled up in a ball as she heard Sam's door shut. Then silent tears tracked down her cheeks as she cried herself to sleep for the first time in a long time.

MOMMY ISN'T HERE. MOMMY isn't coming back. *Scared, and feeling alone, Frankie listened to the adults that were supposed to care for her as they screamed at each other.*

She couldn't understand the words or what they were upset about. She just knew they were mad.

Her foster sister lay on her top bunk reading a magazine with her headphones on. Sarah was used to this and could drown them out. She never played with Frankie. She and Johnny, Sarah's brother, never really acknowledged her. So Frankie lay on the mattress on the floor, curled up in a ball, trying to hold her tears in.

And failing.

No. I'm not a child anymore.

Frankie rolled over on the mattress, and it wasn't her that was crying now. Sitting up, she looked around the small, windowless room. Women of all ages, and colors, sitting on dirty mattresses. Some of the younger ones sniffled.

"What's going to happen to us?" "My mom will be so worried." "I'm scared."

The room began to spin as the faces blurred before her eyes. "Help us."

Frankie awoke with a gasp as Sam shook her shoulder. "Frankie, you're dreaming." Her cheeks sticky with drying tears, Frankie rolled to her back and stared up at him in the darkness. He was kneeling on the floor next to her air mattress. Cupping her face, he gently thumbed the saline trails away. "You were having a nightmare."

It felt like nothing had happened between them earlier that night. And for a second, Frankie almost forgot.

Almost.

"Why do you care?" Her voice came out weak. There was no animosity left tonight, just fatigue.

Sam sighed and ran his hands through his hair. "I... I just do."

Frankie rubbed at her face and looked away. "You say I'm just trying to kill my guilt. But I know what it's like to have no control over your life. To be passed around. And..." she almost choked. "I'm *female*, damn it. Why do you think they tell girls to go to the bathroom in packs? We learn from a young age that there are twisted people out there that will do that shit to us, and we have to protect ourselves." She shivered, despite being under the blanket. "We have to protect each other."

The one thing her group home had taught her was that even if they couldn't trust each other much, they could trust the outside world even less.

Sam squeezed her arm. "I'm sorry. It's just... I care about you. But I care about the law, too."

Well, that was that, then.

"I'm going back to sleep now."

He didn't move from her side. "Do you want me to stay?"

She shrugged. "You don't have to." She didn't need him. She didn't need anyone, damn it.

Sam hesitated, then slipped behind her under the covers. "How about I hold you until you fall back asleep?"

That sounded... amazing. "Suit yourself." But with his warm weight cradling her, and his arm over her stomach, Frankie fell into a dreamless sleep with no effort.

SHE AWOKE THE NEXT morning to Jenna knocking on her door. "Coffee's on."

"Be down in a bit," she croaked. God, she usually only felt this shitty after a night of drinking.

She hesitated at the door to the bathroom. The last thing she wanted to do was face Sam this morning. But it would have to happen, eventually. Still, she'd like to put herself somewhat together before it did.

Frankie gently tapped her fist against the door. No answer. She released a sigh of relief, then slowly opened the door.

The door to Sam's room was wide open, with Sam nowhere in sight. He must have worked out in the basement gym like he usually did. She hastened to shut his door and locked it for good measure. Then she went about her usual morning routine.

Once she'd dressed, Frankie shuffled down the stairs, the smell of coffee already starting to wake her up. Jenna and Roger sat at the island with bowls of cereal.

"Sorry, I didn't sleep well last night, and I didn't think it was smart to try to cook in this case."

Frankie waved away his concerns. "Nothing to apologize for. Cereal is fine with me. What are the options?"

"Honey Nut or plain." Jenna pointed at the boxes on the counter. "I wanted him to get something fun, but Mr. Health Conscious here wouldn't hear of it."

"You can buy whatever cereal you want, Princess. I didn't get your sugar bombs because you didn't text until I was already on the way home."

Frankie smiled as she poured her breakfast into a bowl, glad *some* things around here hadn't changed overnight. Just as she sat down and went to pour her milk, Sam stomped up the basement stairs. He appeared at the cellar door, tank top dark with sweat, wiping at his face with a towel.

"Come on and eat, Sam."

Sam said nothing, but his scowl spoke for itself. He poured a bowl of plain O's and added milk, then leaned against the sink. Close, but not technically eating with them.

Frankie pinched the bridge of her nose. Why couldn't he put on his big boy pants and deal with the emotions later?

Once they all had food, Roger started talking. "I did a lot of thinking last night and not much sleeping. But the conclusion I came to is that we're going to have to watch the house the old-fashioned way. I don't think Frankie should access the cameras until we're going in. So we'll have to stake it out."

"That's dangerous, Roger. You don't want to be too close to them." Jenna bit her lip. If Frankie was Jenna, she'd be worried, too.

"That's what binoculars and camouflage are for, Princess," Roger said after he finished chewing. "Don't worry. I ordered a pop-up hunting blind from the sports store. They won't have any idea we're there."

"We?" Frankie raised an eyebrow at him.

"We're going to take shifts." He pulled out his phone and pulled the area up on his map. "There's an access road back here, and with my military binoculars, we'll be nearly a half mile away. If you see anything," he addressed both the girls, "text me and then get the hell out of there."

Jenna nodded. "And once we know they're there, we spring the girls. Or guys." Jenna quickly corrected herself.

Sam slammed his bowl down on the island. "Come again?"

Sweat beaded on Roger's upper lip. "You said we needed evidence."

"Evidence! A hair, photos not stolen from their servers, an eyewitness! Not a vigilante rescue mission!"

"How is this any different from Columbia, Sam?"

Sam shook his head. "We had orders in Columbia. A clear chain of command that absolved us of any crimes."

"Maybe I answer to a higher chain of command now."

Frankie's eyes went back and forth like a ping-pong ball. She wasn't sure what had happened in Columbia, but she decided the less she knew, the better. Slipping her bowl into the dishwasher, Frankie crept back upstairs to use her remote access for the last time. She'd destroy that video and pray it didn't pop up again later.

Chapter 22

Once the girls disappeared, Roger really let him have it.

"You wanna back out now, asshole? After making such a big show of being all in?"

Sam's chest tightened and his palms stung from his nails digging in. "How did you expect me to react to this, Roger? Forgive everything and sing Kumbaya around the fire pit?"

"No, this is exactly what I expected, which is why *I didn't tell you!*"

That... that hurt even worse. After all their years serving together, that Roger would choose his girl over his brother. Sam staggered into a chair, scrubbing his hands over his face. The stabbing pain in his chest wasn't going away anytime soon.

Roger took advantage of his silence. "What happened to, 'I have to go through too much red tape to get anything done at work,' and 'This sounds more like the good old days.,' huh? You gonna just forget that Frankie was the one who found those pictures and came running for help? I don't know Frankie's story and neither does Jenna, but there's a reason she ended up in that syndicate and it wasn't for kicks, it was for *survival*."

Frankie's words over the course of their short time together came back to him. After her mother died from an overdose, she ended up in foster care, and never finished school from what she'd said. As a teacher, his mother had talked about kids like her when he was growing up. *I think the term is "at risk,"* he thought to himself.

A lump formed in his throat, and he set his head in his hands. "I took an oath, Roger."

"What oath?"

He hadn't had to swear it since he joined the FBI, but he'd been at other swearing-ins and knew the words by rote. "I will support and defend the Constitution of the United States against all enemies, foreign and domestic; that I will bear true faith and allegiance to the same; that I take this obligation freely, without any mental reservation or purpose of evasion; and that I will well and faithfully discharge the duties of the office on which I am about to enter. So help me God."

Sam was pretty sure even God couldn't help him now.

"Not turning in the girls when I know they are some of the criminals the FBI is looking for is a direction violation of that oath."

Roger sighed and scrubbed a hand over his hair. "I understand now." He joined Sam on a bar stool and crossed his arms over his chest. "But they're not the enemy anymore."

"I *know* that." Sam rubbed at his chest over where his heart ached. His feelings for Frankie... "What am I supposed to do?"

"I'm sorry, Sam," he said. "But I can't let you send my girl to prison."

And Sam couldn't in good conscience send Frankie, either.

Life had always seemed so black and white. Bad guys, good guys. Criminals, and non-criminals. But here were two criminals who didn't just give up their lives of crime but were trying to do something to rectify what they'd done. Sam clutched at his head as his worldview cracked, starting to break open.

He had a lot of thinking to do. And he needed time. "I'll take the first shift. I can at least do that much."

Roger nodded. "I'll go with you to set up. Jenna's going to try to go back to sleep so she can take the night shift."

Sam made sure his phone had charged overnight and then met Roger at the truck. They'd borrowed Finn's for the week from Roger's parents' house, something Roger had mentioned each of the siblings did from time to time, so it didn't sit and rot.

Roger drove his Silverado, and Sam drove the Ford F-150 to the access road that ran into the woods. Then they threw tarps on the trucks and hiked to the spot Roger had marked on his GPS.

The pop-up blind went up smoothly, and Roger set a camping chair inside. He'd even bought a tripod for the binoculars, so they aimed them at the syndicate's hideout. Sam wouldn't miss a thing.

Roger stood inside the blind, which didn't really have room for two grown men and a camping chair. But Sam stood there, too, the chair between them.

"I'm sorry, Sam. I didn't know about the oath, but after our time in the Army, I should have guessed they made you swear something like that." He took a deep breath. "It's just, I love that little spitfire, and I know she's not the person she was when she joined that group. She was driven into it in desperation."

Sam pulled his glasses off and scrubbed a hand over his face. "I want to understand."

Roger shrugged. "She told me they recruited her from a soup kitchen. A fucking *soup kitchen*, Sam. That's how down on her luck she was. When she refused to go home and got kicked out of school, she was living under an overpass. They're not bad people. They were just in a desperate situation and the syndicate took advantage of that."

With that, Roger gripped his shoulder in farewell and headed back to his truck.

Hours passed. God, he'd forgotten how fucking mind-numbing these types of operations could be. The cries of birds in the surrounding trees were his only soundtrack. At one point, he saw a raccoon lumbering through the brush.

All he had for company were his thoughts. He hadn't even wanted to download an audiobook for fear of missing something. Now he regretted it.

Thoughts of Frankie swirled through his mind. *The University of Hard Knocks,* she'd said. *She overdosed when I was little. I don't remember much before I went into the foster system.*

His mom used to talk about one particular student who lashed out at all the other teachers, except her. He loved math and would hang out in her classroom as often as possible, helping the other kids and working in the extra workbooks she kept in the back. *I know he's behind on his other studies*, he remembered her saying one night, *but when he acts out all the teachers just send him to me because he behaves for me.*

In the end, someone finally got him tested and discovered the student had severe dyslexia. Then it all fell into place.

Mom had taught in the inner city schools and her kids didn't always have the best home life. That kid had parents who didn't even notice the problem enough to get him tested until he was a teen. By which point, he'd already fallen far behind in most subjects. Another student needed glasses, and one teacher finally had to take her to an eye doctor to get her examined. Because her mother couldn't be bothered.

Sam scowled into the woods. Frankie didn't even remember her mother except that she'd been a druggie. And foster care wasn't all rainbows and butterflies. One of the true crime shows he'd watched with Roger in the barracks came to mind. A serial killer had hunted foster children because "no one would miss them." Trafficking a foster kid could be easy for the same reason. It could easily have been Frankie in those photos as well.

And Frankie had been so young. All the things your parents were supposed to do when you were small, like tuck you in, kiss you goodnight... she wouldn't have had that. He'd had a mom that read him bedtime stories and dragged him to church on Sundays. When his dad was home, he had a solid, male role model. She might not have had the direction to know stealing and hacking was wrong. Hell, from what she'd hinted at, she'd been in survival mode all her life. *I don't make plans, Sam. No expectations, no pain.* She'd had no choice.

Just like Roger said, Jenna had no choice.

Damn, Sam was in trouble. Because the girl he'd been falling for had been the hacker he'd sought all along, and there was no way he could turn her in, or Jenna for that matter. How could he fault them, if, like Roger said, it had all been for survival?

Suddenly, the world wasn't so black and white anymore.

But he didn't dare share this realization with anyone until after his turn at the stakeout. Sam wiped the sweat from his forehead. It was hot in this little tent. The mesh ventilation windows were not enough to keep his body from heating the whole thing like an oven. Every time a cool breeze blew through the hunting blind, he wanted to cry with relief.

Only four more hours to go, then Jenna would arrive when the sun went down.

Movement at the house caught his attention. A fancy car had pulled up to the house. It was at the wrong angle to read the plate, but he lifted his phone and took a picture through the lenses, anyway. An older man got out and walked up to the front door. It opened, but the occupant stayed in the shadows while the guest went inside.

He snapped another photo, then waited. The sun had dipped further in the sky when the older man exited the house, but he wasn't alone.

Sam immediately started shooting a video. A young man followed behind the guest, head down, hair long and un-kempt. The only reason Sam was sure it was a male was because he wore no shirt. The older man opened the back door and when he turned to show the younger man inside, Sam realized the young one's hands were bound.

This was not some sexy foreplay, like he'd done with Frankie. Even at this distance, he could see the young man trembling.

Once the car drove off and Sam stopped the recording, he texted Roger.

> **Sam:** They're in there. No idea how they got in, but I just saw a guy go in alone, then leave with someone.

> **Roger: Probably that slip in the back we saw on the map.**

> **Sam:** This shit is creepy. But I got a video.

> **Roger: Good job. I'll tell Jenna we're moving tonight.**

> **Sam:** Don't tell Frankie I lost one.

> **Roger: Once your boys in the Bureau get involved, they'll track him down.**

> **Sam:** I hope so. I tried to get the license plate.

> **Roger: Pack it in and come on back. Are you sure about this?**

Sam considered Roger's question for a moment. He could send this video to Ross, tell him what he suspected, and let the FBI handle it from there. But something about knowing there were more people trapped inside, slated for a fate like the young man he'd been too far away to save, flipped a switch inside.

> Sam: I'm all in, brother.

FRANKIE HATED WAITING AROUND. Jenna was asleep, to prepare for her stakeout shift that night, and Roger was in his office taking care of administrative work.

When Roger got back from setting Sam up at the stakeout point, he'd found her packing her bags and boxing up her monitors. He'd told her that he had talked to Sam, and that he was working to find a way to keep her and Jenna safe. Frankie wasn't sure she could trust Roger to help *her*, but she knew there was no way he'd ever let anything happen to Jenna. So she'd stayed. She'd packed, but she wasn't leaving yet.

She had to see this through, anyway. After Thursday, she'd run again and forget about Sam. The thought of leaving him made her heart ache. And wasn't that something strange? She hadn't felt that way about leaving a place since she was little and bouncing from foster home to foster home.

The thought of leaving Jenna only made it worse.

It wouldn't be the first time she'd disappeared from other people's lives. Growing up in the unique nomadic way of the foster kid had taught her how to make new friends, but not let them get too close. She'd known so many people over the years she couldn't remember all their names. But no one had lasted as long as Jenna. Granted, they'd been work acquaintances and hadn't even known each other's real names most of that time. Yet they'd gotten close all the same, somehow.

Jenna was her best friend, but Frankie wasn't sure she could ever look Sam in the eye again. Once this mission was over, she was out.

Standing on Roger's porch, she looked at the clear blue sky and knew exactly what she needed. She slipped back into the house, headed to Roger's first floor den he'd set up as an office, and knocked on the open door.

"Hey, Frankie, what's up?" Roger looked up from his computer screen.

"I just wanted to let someone know I'm going out for a ride. Especially after last time."

"I'd steer clear of the industrial side of town," he said with a chuckle. "But thanks for the heads up. When will you be back?"

"Hopefully by the time Jenna is awake. Want me to pick anything up for dinner?"

"No, I think I have everything we need. But thanks."

"Sure, no problem. I'll see you later."

"Be safe, Frankie."

She laced up her boots and tightened her helmet, then strode out the front door to her beloved bike. It didn't take her long to find the entrance to one of the scenic byways. She didn't need to disturb a residential neighborhood, she just wanted to ride.

It might be September, but fall hadn't come to Charm City just yet. Having lived in the desert all her life, the cooler fall temperatures were a relief to her already, even if her hair hated the humidity. She wasn't looking forward to winter, but she'd survive.

Winter? Where had that thought come from? Frankie didn't know if she'd still be here come winter, or if the syndicate would get their way and put her in the ground. Or maybe Sam would turn her into the FBI, and she'd end up in federal prison.

Damn, this entire operation had her more nervous than she realized. She shook her head free of the depressing thoughts. Once the victims were safe, and the syndicate was no more, then she could think about a future.

Although based on his behavior the night before, that future would *not* be with Sam.

Frankie swallowed past the lump in her throat at the memory of his ice-cold stare when he'd discovered what the rest of them had been hiding from him. It sucked that they had to lie by omission, but she felt better knowing he was aware of it. Unfortunately, that didn't keep her warm last night.

One of the consequences of not letting anyone close was the fact she hadn't been in a long-term relationship before. And while she'd been telling herself she was just a vacation fling for him, he'd all but told her he was coming back and wanted her to stick around. When he'd asked if she wanted anything for herself, her heart had an answer that she couldn't speak out loud. That's why she'd changed the subject so quickly.

She'd wanted to answer, "You."

But the chances of Sam being hers had disappeared with his trust. She took a hand off the grip to rub at the knot forming at her sternum. Movement in her rearview mirror caught her eye. A black SUV was coming up behind her.

This was the first car she'd seen on the road so far, which didn't surprise her since it was the middle of a random Tuesday. Most people were at work or school right now. So then, what was this guy's hurry? Frankie moved to the side of the lane to let him pass more easily. No one was coming in the opposite lane, so he'd have plenty of room.

Frankie's eyes flicked between the mirror and the road, bracing herself for the rush of wind sure to come when he passed her. But that wasn't what the SUV did.

They were getting closer and not moving around her at all. She was heading around a mountain now, a guardrail up ahead around the steepest drop. But no guardrail stood between her and the woods that lead downhill.

Her eyes widened as she watched it happen, helpless to do anything but swerve.

The driver didn't even touch the brakes. She didn't hear the telltale squeal, anyway. Not over the sound of their grill hitting her fender. She swerved the bike at the last minute, in total disbelief that this idiot wouldn't just go around. When he smacked into her bike again, only harder, she knew it was no accident. They were trying to kill her!

Frankie released the clutch and let the bike coast toward the woods, hoping to direct it away from any large trees. The bumpy ground threw off her balance, and the bike rolled with her on top of it. She rolled too, jumping off the motorcycle at the last second and tucking her arms in so she could get as far away as possible.

She came to a stop when she rolled into a bush, then pushed herself underneath it as far as she could go. Thorns snagged at her clothes, and her whole body was going to feel like one enormous bruise, but she was alive.

Silence descended as she waited for the other shoe to drop. Would they turn around to finish the job? Or was that enough to make them think she was dead? Or maybe killing her hadn't been on the agenda. They just wanted to hurt her.

As she lay there, listening to the wind blow through the trees, she realized the most likely explanation, provided this had been the syndicate, was that the minions had wanted to get the job done quickly. They had probably figured if they caught her out like this, she would die regardless, and it would look like an accident of her own making. *Clever assholes,* she thought to herself.

When she decided the SUV wasn't making a return trip, she crawled out from under the bush and stifled a groan. Riding back was going to hurt like a motherfucker, but if her bike was usable, she wanted to do it.

Fuck them and the horse they rode in on. She'd leave under her own power just to prove they hadn't hurt her.

She forced her way back up the steep hill. Ugh, her knee was out of whack and she should probably get an X-ray. But hospitals and information and... ugh. That was a Future Frankie problem. Present Frankie had to focus on getting back to a safe place.

Her poor bike was definitely worse for wear. It was still running, so Frankie turned the key and the motor shut off. She grabbed onto the handlebars and pulled the bike around so it was pointing up the hill, back toward the road.

Then, she stopped to catch her breath and listened to the woods again. Still nothing. That didn't mean they weren't going to go back to look for her body. Or call in the accident anonymously.

She had to get home before anyone else came by.

She thanked her lucky stars her saddlebags were empty. Holding onto the handlebar with her right hand, her knees protested as she squatted down, perching her rear end on the edge of the seat. Then, taking baby steps and going as fast as her aching body allowed, she pushed the motorcycle up and kicked the stand down.

Okay, she was back in business. Frankie took another quick breather, her ears open for any sounds of traffic. The buzz of a car made her pause, but only the small red flash of a sedan zooming by.

Despite her body's soreness, Frankie climbed back on the bike and turned the ignition. Her alignment was likely shot to hell, but at least she could get back.

Chapter 23

Sam sat outside talking to his mom on the phone when Frankie returned. Her bike looked like it had been on the losing side of some kind of argument. The fender folded in on itself to the point he wouldn't expect the back wheel to turn. Both rider and motorcycle were smudged with dirt, and a couple of twigs poked out from between the panels.

"Hey, Mom? I gotta go."

"Okay, Son. Have a good rest of your trip. Wish me luck at bingo tonight!"

"Good luck, Mom. Love you." He didn't wait to hear her return the sentiment and hung up as he watched

Frankie struggle to get off her motorcycle. Before he realized he'd even stood up, he found himself crossing the lawn to get to her as she stumbled toward the house.

"What the hell happened to you?"

She flipped her visor up. "Some asshole ran me off the road."

"Holy shit." He looked her over from head to toe. Her leather jacket was scuffed to hell, tears in the fabric across her back. It looked as though her jeans had torn in a couple places as well, the skin underneath red and angry. "Let's get you inside."

"I need to ask Roger if I can put my bike in the garage. They came at me from behind."

Sam nodded. "I'll ask him to put it inside. No need to advertise where you're staying." He held his arms out to help her up the stairs, but she ignored them. Stubborn thing. But he knew he deserved it. He'd been an ass. He held the door open for her, anyway.

"I'll ask Roger where the first aid kit is and meet you in our bathroom."

Frankie groaned in protest. "I'm fine."

"You're really not." She was likely still riding high off the adrenaline, but she'd certainly feel it in the morning.

"I'm just bruised."

"I'm not so sure." He paused as she started hauling herself up the staircase. "If you'd rather ask Jenna..."

"Yeah, I would," she snapped.

He raised his hands in surrender. "Okay. I'll send her up." He left Frankie to go find Roger and Jenna in the kitchen.

Roger looked up from a plate he had piled with raw burgers. "Hey, Frankie back yet?"

"Yeah, but it's not good."

Jenna paused in mixing the pasta salad. "What's wrong?"

Sam sighed. He'd rather be the one checking Frankie out, just to assure himself she was all in one piece. But she'd asked for Jenna. "Jenna, can you take the first aid kit up to her? Someone ran her off the road."

She dropped her spoon with a gasp. "Right away." She reached under the kitchen sink and removed a white box, then bolted for the upstairs bathroom. "Bitch, you got some 'splainin' to do!"

Roger stood there, stunned. "Is she okay?"

Sam shrugged. "She's alive, and appears to be in one piece, if that's what you're asking. Do you mind moving her motorcycle into the garage? She said whoever did it came up behind her, and we don't want to advertise she made it home."

"Yeah, we can do that. You know the code. Just open the door and wheel it in."

"Thanks, man."

Sam knocked on the island and left to take care of Frankie's bike. The sun was starting to sink in the sky. He plugged the code into the number pad next to the garage door and it opened for him. Putting her motorcycle in gear, he grabbed the handlebars and kicked up the stand, then carefully wheeled it backward into the bay next to Roger's Silverado. The rear was bent to shit, and the frame didn't want to move in a straight line. She was going to need a lot of work to get it back in tip-top shape again. How the hell had she ridden back on this thing? He shook his head, knowing her stubbornness was the answer.

The smell of flame-grilled meat filled the air. Roger must have started dinner. After putting the door back down, he walked around to the back porch where Roger stood sipping a soda next to his grill.

"How's the bike?"

"Not great." He sat down at the wooden picnic table. "I don't know how she got it home other than sheer force of will. It's going to need body work and an alignment at best."

Roger let out a whistle. "I'm curious to hear everything that happened."

"You and me both, brother." That's when Jenna appeared at the back door with the pasta salad in her hands. Sam stood at once to get the door for her. Behind her limped Frankie, the sides of her face already starting to swell. She had the buns and the condiments, as well as an ice pack.

Jenna laid the bowl down, then helped Frankie unload. Frankie sat down on the bench with a groan and laid the ice pack on her knee.

"What the hell happened?" Roger asked her, splitting his attention between Frankie and the burgers.

Jenna put her hand up. "Give me a sec to get the plates and everything out here, then she only has to tell it once."

"I'll help you, Jenna." Sam said and followed her inside. Together, they carted out plates, napkins, cans of soda, and silverware. Jenna even remembered the serving spoon for the salad.

Roger tested the burgers, then put the lid down on the grill and turned around. "Okay, we're all here. Can you tell us what happened?"

Frankie sighed. "I was driving along the scenic by-way, going around the mountain. I hadn't seen many cars. There was this black SUV that came up behind me. He was doing way over the speed limit. No one was on the other side, so I moved to the edge to let him pass me.

But he wasn't interested in passing me. He tapped my rear fender, twice, and the second time was so hard I had to drive over the hill to get away." At Jenna's gasp, she patted her shoulder to reassure her. "If he'd waited thirty more seconds, I would have been sandwiched between him and the guardrail."

"Jesus, Frankie. You could have died!" Sam scrubbed a hand over his face, grateful he was sitting down for this story.

"Yeah, I know. I think that was their intention. So anyway, I'm losing control. I veer the bike off into the woods and down the slightly less steep side of the mountain, and then the bike rolls. I had to jump off, or it would have squished my leg, and I just let myself keep rolling down hill to try to get away in case they came after me. When I stopped, and realized they weren't coming back, I picked my bike up and got the fuck out of there."

Sam's heart raced as he thought about Frankie out there, alone and in danger. He looked away as Jenna enveloped her in the hug he wanted desperately to give her. But he'd lost that privilege.

His soda can crunched in his hand. Recovering, he opened it and took a careful sip. The release of the pressure popped the can back to its correct shape.

"It's a good thing we're going in tonight."

Frankie's head snapped to look at her friend. "What do you mean, we're going in tonight?"

Roger and Jenna both shook their heads. "Not you, Frankie. You need to heal," said Jenna.

If looks could kill, Jenna wouldn't be sitting in front of him anymore. "What changed?"

Sam cleared his throat. "I saw movement today on the stakeout. They're in the house."

Frankie's shoulders sank. "And you don't want to give them a chance to leave."

"Right." Roger walked over carrying a steaming plate of perfectly grilled burgers. "I'm sorry, Frankie. But if they're escalating, we need to move now."

"You're right. And I'll only slow you all down." She propped her elbow on the table and laid her head on her fist.

"You'll be much more helpful behind the screen. You always were the best at that."

Jenna slipped a burger on Frankie's plate and then passed the platter to Sam. She laid a hand on Frankie's. "You're not in this alone."

Frankie smiled at her friend as he took a patty for himself and then passed the meat back to Roger. "If we can crack the code on those documents, maybe they'll help us track everyone down."

His sweetness set her jaw and looked up at him. Fuck, he needed to apologize. But later. In private. For now, Sam occupied himself with prepping his bun.

Roger had been right. He couldn't turn these two in. He'd sooner cut off his own arm than turn in the feisty woman trying to save these victims. She deserved a medal, not jail time. Hopefully, she kept herself clean after this. Maybe he could even give her a reason to?

That made him think about the information Frankie and Jenna had about the syndicate. With the evidence the girls could give the FBI, they'd be one hell of an asset. Maybe he could work out some immunity deal with Ross's supervisor.

Chapter 24

Frankie sat behind Roger's computer with her headset on. They'd agreed that getting into the syndicate's cameras from her laptop would be suicide, so she'd installed some of her software onto his tower. The Alienware had already proven far faster than her machine. She tried to tamp down the jealousy.

Roger had purchased earpieces for all of them, the same type as Jenna had used to communicate with Frankie when she'd stolen for the syndicate. They'd left the dishes in the sink after their early dinner to get all the installing done on this machine.

For now, she was alone with her thoughts as her friends traveled to the syndicate's hideaway. She laid her head back against the chair with a heavy sigh, wishing she could have gone with them. Her hands itched to get dirty, but as Roger pointed out, she'd never fired a gun. Jenna also knew how good she was at helping her dodge security during a heist, so she'd agreed to stay behind. Plus, she was injured, and she couldn't afford to slow them down. The pain reliever she'd swallowed had taken the edge off her bruised feeling, but she knew it would be back with a vengeance later.

She'd promised Jenna that if she was still limping to-morrow, she'd go with her to a clinic to get an X-ray.

Thinking about Sam and her friends putting themselves in danger made her chew at her nails. She had to fight to keep herself from hacking into the cameras too early. If they tipped someone off, it would only hurt them in the long run. And with her limp, pacing was out of the question. She found herself tapping on the desk to get the nervous energy out.

Ugh, this was taking forever!

Finally, Jenna's voice chirped in her ear. "Hey, Frankie, we're almost there."

"Okay, everyone, check in and make sure the earpiece is working."

Sam's voice was the next one in her ear, and it made her stomach do flips. Even if all he was saying was "Ivers, checking in." Damn, she'd miss him when he was gone.

"Hunt, checking in."

"Alright, I got all of you. Can you all hear me?"

Sam was the first to answer. "Yep."

"Affirmative." That was Roger. "Stealth mode engaged." Roger must have turned the headlights off.

"Okay, Frankie, get eyes on the place. We're coming up the street now."

Frankie immediately gained access to the cameras attached to the house, and started looping the feeds so no one would know anything was wrong. First, she focused on the outer cameras and saw the black SUV Roger had rented driving slowly along the road.

"I have the visual. You're far enough away that you should be good to disembark."

"I'll drive into that clearing we saw on the satellite, and then we can throw the camo tarp over the car."

This was great. It was almost as though she rode along with them.

Two car doors opened, and then Sam spoke. "Frankie, when I get back, we need to talk."

She bristled in her seat. "I don't think there's anything to talk about."

He sighed. "That came out wrong. I mean, I need to talk to you. In private. I can't... I can't say it with everyone listening. And there wasn't time after dinner."

Frankie's brows furrowed. "Alright. But focus on the mission or you won't get the chance."

Once Sam was out of the car, they threw the tarp over-top the vehicle, and it disappeared into the trees that stood between it and the camera she watched.

"You guys are good."

They'd all put on face paint before leaving, with Jenna in her catsuit and Sam and Roger in their decommissioned ACUs and helmets. As they approached the house from the woods, Frankie flicked through the screens to see what was going on inside the house.

Something was wrong. There weren't many people inside the house, just a few goons. When she got to the bedroom, that's where she found the women.

"I've got four guys, one with a gun, and about ten women inside the house. They must not put them all in one place at a time.""Makes sense. What kind of gun?"

"A big one." Frankie didn't know shit about guns, damn it! "What's going on out there? They're rounding the women up and forcing them to walk."

Jenna's whisper was frantic. "Guys, the dock!"

Frankie quickly brought up the camera that faced the river. A small boat had pulled in with its lights out to avoid detection. "They're moving them!" Great, this just proved the card had been a setup. The date of the "auction" should have been tomorrow. If they'd come when they were told, they'd have been too late.

Or maybe that was just how the syndicate vetted potential customers.

"It's show time," said Roger.

"There's gonna be more guns on that boat," Sam reminded him.

Frankie swallowed back the bile that tried to rise in her throat. Images of her friends and lover, bloodied and beaten, assaulted her mind's eye. And she'd have no way of helping them!

Trying to calm her breathing, she couldn't take her eyes off the screen as her friends flattened themselves to hide behind the tall grass. Thank goodness the syndicate didn't care about appearances.

One of the syndicate goons stepped outside the house, blinking a flashlight in some kind of code at the guy tying the boat to the dock. There were no lights out here besides the glow coming from the back door. The guard didn't have night vision like the security cameras did, so he didn't see their crew laying in wait. When he turned back to go inside, Sam rushed him and knocked him off his feet into the grass on the other side, his hand over his mouth. But someone fired a shot from the boat and then all hell broke loose.

Roger fired back at the boat, and a crack of glass shattered the silence. The boat driver let out a string of shots, but Roger didn't stay in one place. He kept moving, and so did Jenna. She could barely make them out on the camera, so she knew whoever was out there couldn't see them at all.

Meanwhile, Sam wrestled with the syndicate guard, popping in and out of her view. He gritted his pearly white teeth, a stark contrast to his face paint, as he wrapped his arm around the guy's neck and took him to the ground. A couple thuds later, and Sam popped back up alone.

"Is he..."

Sam just shook his head directly at the camera. They must have discussed no killing in the raid tonight. After all, if anyone called the cops, they were technically in the wrong. No matter what criminals had hidden in the house.

Frankie flipped back and forth between the two cameras, trying to use what came through the earpiece and the bits she could catch from the stationary cameras to figure out what was going on. Then the other goons ran out of the house, the armed one with his gun raised to his shoulder.

"Two more just came out!"

Roger took aim and fired, and she winced at the shot echoing in her ear. The armed one dropped his gun and screamed. Realizing he was out of the fight, he ran for the boat.

The other one saw what had happened to his friend, realized how close to the house Sam was, then turned and jumped him before she could warn him, wrestling him back to the ground. Roger grabbed the rifle on the ground and took aim at the boat operator. He ducked behind the wooden path that led to the bay when the driver fired back.

"Our orders were to move it! Let's go!" The wounded thug shouted over the noise.

Sam's wrestling partner kneed him in the groin, then ran back inside. Sam went down. Frankie bit her tongue. *Damn it, I need those later!*

Her heart nearly stopped. She... she *wanted* to work things out with Sam. Her breathing came fast. She loved him? Fuck, she *loved* him!

Hell of a time to have a revelation, Frankie! Get your head in the game!

That's when she realized Jenna had crept around the side and out of her sight range, headed for the front of the house as they planned. The syndicate had installed a digital lock to avoid having to give the key out, and she easily deactivated it so Jenna could open it.

"I'm going in," Jenna whispered.

"Got it, Jenna." Frankie answered her.

"Who the fuck are you?" Shit! Henchman number four! And she didn't have a camera on the foyer! The familiar sound of a switchblade cut through the night. Thuds and grunts and a boat motor were all she could hear. She didn't know if it was Jenna or Sam or Roger!

Frankie gripped the arms of the desk chair so hard her knuckles turned nearly white. She had to keep her head in the game. They needed her to be their secret weapon.

They needed body cameras, damn it!

The sounds of a fight eased, and she silently gasped for air.

"Jenna! Do you need backup?"

"Negative. He's gone." The sound of footsteps running away came from Jenna's mic. "What's the upstairs look like?"

Frankie flitted through the upstairs cameras. "Nothing. It's empty. Damn it!" She pounded her fist against the desk. Flipping back to the backyard view, she watched with a sinking heart as the last henchman, holding a nose streaming blood, herded a line of shivering, barely clothed women along the dock to the boat. Sam and Roger were nowhere to be seen.

Air evaporated from her lungs as her whole body seized with fear. "Sam! Roger! Come in!" Her voice trembled. "Are you guys okay?"

Panting came over her headphones, but Roger was the first to speak. "We're both going to be sore, but yeah, I think we're okay."

"Where the fuck are you? I can't see you."

"Under the boardwalk." Roger gasped. "Fuck, I'm too old for this shit."

"Pretty sure I have a bruised rib," Sam countered with a grunt. "One of those bullets got me in the vest."

"What about your balls?" She found herself asking.

He huffed a laugh. "You worried about them?"

Shit. She hadn't meant to show her hand like that. "It looked painful."

"Coulda been worse," he answered. "I'm wearing a cup."

"Smart." Frankie did one last cycle through all the interior cameras. "The house is clear." She told them, her voice flat.

"Jenna, that last guy came running out with a bloody nose. Was that you?" Pride shone in Roger's voice.

"You know it. Brass knuckles for the win." Frankie couldn't help but grin at that. "What happened?" Jenna asked.

"They got the captives out. I saw them marching the women down to the boat." Frankie sighed, her disappointment bleeding through her voice. "We failed, Jenna."

"Not quite," came Jenna's voice. "Someone was dragging one of them down the stairs when I got in... I'm not sure if she's..." A groan came through her earpiece, and then Jenna appeared in the camera from the front door and turned it around so Frankie could see.

On a linoleum foyer floor that had seen better days, a woman in a threadbare dress lay on her stomach. Slowly the survivor rolled to her back, as if in pain. Pale hair that desperately needed a brush lay underneath her. Once she rolled over, Frankie could see her skin hung loosely from her frame, and the dress didn't hide that her collarbones were far too pronounced to be getting regular meals. Squinting, she shielded her eyes from Jenna's flashlight.

Immediately Jenna flipped the flashlight up into her own face. "It's okay. I'm here to rescue you."

Frankie slumped back in the chair, all the tension gone from her muscles. Her eyes prickled, and she blinked rapidly. This was why she'd endured the nightmares, why she'd worked so hard behind the scenes. They'd pulled it off. Not to the extent she'd hoped, but they'd gotten one away from the clutches of the syndicate. Frankie muted herself as the tears flowed freely. She sobbed into her hands, both from relief, and for the women they'd failed.

Chapter 25

SAM WORKED HIS JAW back and forth as he slid his helmet off. That was definitely going to bruise. He pushed his tongue against his teeth, but didn't find any loose ones. Phew.

They'd ducked under the boardwalk to avoid getting shot, which was when the women had rushed out. That's when they knew they had lost. The goons wouldn't care if the women got shot, but he and Roger did.

He'd only half paid attention to what Jenna was saying up to now, but then he heard his name.

"Okay, so outside is my boyfriend, Roger, and his friend, Sam. They look like big meanies, but they're good guys."

"O-okay." Another voice trembled, and he looked at Roger, his brows furrowed in confusion.

"They left one behind," Roger mouthed at him.

Sam's jaw dropped. Then his knees buckled from pain and shock. He caught himself and bent over, his hands on his knees and his breaths coming in gasps. Roger patted him on the back, and he stood back up. He'd been gearing himself up to face Frankie in utter failure. It wasn't the outcome they'd wanted, but he'd take it.

Ross was going to chew his ass out, but it would be worth it.

Jenna appeared at the back door, which still hung open. Behind her, walking on shaky legs, was a ghost. She'd gone pale from lack of sunlight, her face so thin her eyes looked too big for her head. The poor thing clung to Jenna's arm, and when he looked at what she was wearing, he realized she was barefoot.

"Gentlemen, this is Josie. Josie, this is my boyfriend Roger, and his best friend, Sam." The men waved in turn.

Sam approached her slowly. "Jenna, she can't walk to the car like that. Her feet..." Jenna looked down, and it seemed for the first time she realized the survivor had no shoes.

"Shit. I don't think we should move the car. The less footage Frankie has to delete, the better."

Frankie sounded in their ears. "The house is clear. And yeah, if you can get her to the car without crossing the line of sight again, that would be great. But I'll make it work."

"Hey, Frankie," Roger said into his earpiece. "Change the codes on the doors, okay? We want the FBI to get as much evidence as possible."

"You got it."

Josie quivered in the chill night air. The syndicate had only given her a threadbare sundress. She had to be freezing. Sam furrowed his brow in concern. "Josie, how about I carry you over to our car and we get out of here?"

Jenna kept talking. "You're welcome to stay with us if you want, or we can try to get you home."

Josie shook her head. "I don't even know where I am. They didn't tell us where they were taking us."

"You're in Baltimore, Maryland." Jenna told her, and Josie responded with a sob.

"It's so far…"

Jenna wrapped an arm around her. "Let's get you somewhere safe for now. We can figure out the details later."

Sam turned his back and crouched. Jenna helped Josie get on his back, piggyback style. Then the four of them made their way back through the tall grass to the woods where the SUV lay camouflaged. Roger pulled the tarp off and stuffed it back into the trunk, where he proceeded to secure his weapons. Sam crouched again so Josie wouldn't hit her head, and only once she was in the vehicle did he realize there was blood in her hair.

He reached out and probed it gently. "We should take you to the hospital."

Her lower lip trembled. "One of them hit me in the head and I passed out. When I woke up, Jenna was there. And everyone else was gone."

Sam looked at Roger. "She could have a concussion. We need a professional."

Roger looked down at himself. "We can't go in there looking like this."

Jenna pulled makeup wipes out of her bag in the back. "Here, boys. This will help. We should stop at home and find her some shoes. And a sweater."

"Good idea." Frankie's voice in his ear made him jump. "You should all change clothes when you get back and then someone can take her to the hospital. I think she'd be more comfortable with Jenna."

"We'll ask. See you at home, Frankie." Jenna took the earpiece out and clicked it off. Sam waited for Roger to the do the same, then he knew the line was private.

"I'll see you soon, sweetness."

She stayed quiet, and he wondered if she was going to respond. "See you when you get here, soldier boy."

FRANKIE MET THEM AT the garage with a pair of Jenna's sandals in her hands. Jenna jumped out of the back of the SUV and took them from her and gave them to Josie. "See if these fit." Sam bit his lip as he and Frankie followed the pair into the house. Roger was right behind them.

"I want one of us to take the SUV back to the rental place first thing in the morning."

Sam nodded. "I think you should go with Jenna and Josie to the hospital. Frankie and I can stay here."

When they reached the living room, Josie was sitting on the couch. Jenna came into the room from the direction of the kitchen, a tall glass of water in her hands. Josie clutched it in both hands like it was gold.

"Don't drink it too fast. You don't want to shock your system." Jenna gestured to them. "This is my friend,

Frankie. She was the one in our earpieces tonight." Frankie waved.

"How about I sit with you while these guys go get cleaned up?"

Josie nodded. Sam was the last to leave them, unwilling to take his eyes off Frankie.

There had been a moment during that fight where he'd wondered if he'd get to see her again. One of the bullets had hit his vest, and the bruise hurt like a motherfucker. When the goons had come out to the yard to fight them directly, he had no idea if they were out of bullets, or whether they had other weapons on them. He knew they wouldn't be that lucky again. The thing with organizations like the syndicate was, they would continue to be one or two steps ahead of them. Cut off one head, and two more would replace it. But the alternative was to give up, and he couldn't do that.

He was a Green Beret, damn it.

Back in his room, Sam stripped his ACUs off and left them in a heap on the floor to deal with later. The makeup wipes Jenna gave them had taken most of the camouflage off, but he hadn't had a mirror, so he'd missed a lot. For instance, he could still see it in the creases around his nose, and it had left a thin layer of greenish gray over his face and neck. Using soap and water at the sink took care of the rest. Then he threw on jeans and a t-shirt and headed downstairs.

Frankie sat alone in the living room. "They left already," she told him.

"Did they find her a jacket or something?" He sat down in the recliner across from her.

"Yeah, Jenna loaned her a hoodie and some leggings." She shook her head. "I can't believe they left her behind."

"I don't think it was intentional." Sam told her, leaning forward on his knees. "She said one of them had knocked her out, and I think we distracted them."

"At least we got one of them out." She looked down at the can of soda in her hand. "I think I need something stronger."

"Not too strong. I still want to talk to you."

Frankie shook her head. "Can it wait until tomorrow?"

Sam glanced away for a moment. "If you sleep in my bed tonight."

When he looked back at her, her lower lip trembled. "Do you mean it?"

He ran a hand through his sweaty hair. Ugh, he was definitely going to shower. "I mean it, sweetness. I'm sorry for reacting the way I did. You're allowed to change, and I appreciate that about you." He paused. "I'll negotiate with the FBI for you and Jenna to get immunity in exchange for the information you have on the syndicate."

"So the fling is back on until you leave?"

Sam shook his head. He'd done a terrible job of explaining himself, as usual. Hopefully, over time, he could learn how to do better. For now, he knew the only way to get Frankie to believe him was to lay himself bare.

"It was never a fling for me, Frankie. Francesca. I had every intention of begging you to stay while I went to pack up my life and move here." Ugh, why had he sat so far away from her?

Frankie chewed at her nails. "I thought you didn't want me once you found out who I was. I was going... to leave."

Time to pay the piper. "I was hurt, and I was upset, and I said a lot of things I regret. But I understand now that the world isn't just black and white. That it's possible to do the wrong thing for the right reason."

She fidgeted on the couch. "I... I don't have many other skills, and I don't know what I'm going to do, Sam."

"It would be my honor to help you use your powers for good, Frankie. What do you say? Will you stay?"

"With you?"

He nodded. "If you want to. I'll be apartment hunting soon anyway, and we'll want to give Jenna and Roger their privacy. But if you want your own place for a while, I'm good with that, too. Whatever you want."

Frankie released a shaky breath. "To be honest, Sam, I've never done this before. I just want you."

"Neither have I, sweetness. We can learn together." He held his arms out, the need to hold her overwhelming. "Come here?"

She nodded her head and stood up as he spoke, rounding the coffee table. When she fell into his arms, he let out a groan.

Immediately, she sat up. "What happened?"

"Sorry, sweetness, you'll have to be gentle with me for a bit. One of their bullets hit my vest, and it hurts."

"Let me see." She tore at his shirt until he grabbed her hands and held them still.

"Upstairs." One word, and she was pulling him out of the chair. Together they strode up the staircase, and an expanding feeling filled his chest with light and heat.

Inside his room, he stripped for her inspection. "I need a shower," he said apologetically.

"Hush. Holy cow, that looks painful."

"I'm probably too old for field work. I think I'll stay behind the screen as much as possible."

"Can't say I'd complain." She leaned forward and traced the edge of the red mark that was already starting to turn purple. "Want some company in there?"

"I'm not sure I'm up to doing much." He shivered under her touch.

"No, that's too acrobatic for tonight. I won't get in the shower with you. I just don't want to let you out of my sight."

He shrugged. "Sure." She followed him into the joined bathroom, and then he pointed at her room. "We should move my stuff in there so Josie can have an actual bed."

Frankie nodded. "They'll be at the hospital all night tonight. So, since we both need to heal, we should take the mattress one last time."

Unable to help himself, he leaned over and kissed her. "You're right. I'll get us a hotel room tomorrow."

She kissed him back until he forgot all about the shower. "Let's get you clean." Smirking, she gestured for him to turn on the water.

The hot water felt like heaven. He washed himself quickly, cataloging sore spots and bruises.

"How's your knee?"

"It's feeling better. The ice helped a lot."

"Good." He hoped the same guys who had been at the house had been the ones to run her off the road. Thinking of how much pain they'd both be in tonight, stuck on that tiny boat with no shower, shouldn't make him chuckle.

"What's so funny?"

"Just thinking about those assholes stuck on a tiny boat with no bathroom tonight."

"I hope they feel it for days."

"Pretty sure Jenna broke a nose tonight. He's definitely going to feel it for a while." He shampooed his hair and rinsed it out. "Can you hand me my towel?"

"Sure, babe."

He shut the water off, and when he emerged, Frankie stood there with his towel in her hands. Instead of letting him take it, she dried him off herself, gently swiping over his skin.

His heart melted. When she was done, she handed it to him. "I'm too short to reach your hair."

Sam scrubbed at his hair, then leaned over to wrap his arms around her and kissed her until they both were senseless. When he finally came up for air, he pressed his forehead to hers and just held her.

"I need you," he murmured.

"Take me to bed, soldier boy."

Chapter 26

Sam peeled her shirt away and cringed at the bandages on her back. "Sweetness, are you sure?"

Frankie hummed as she stroked his strong, lean shoulders. "I'm sure. I need you, too." She unhooked her bra and let it fall to the floor. Sam's eyes and hands fell on her breasts, gently stroking them and rolling his thumbs over her nipples. Frankie bit her lip as the pleasure jolted through her body.

"I don't have a marathon in me tonight, babe." She caught his hand and dragged him to the bedroom. Once next to the bed, she pulled her leggings and panties down her legs. Then she stepped aside and pointed at the bed. "Lay down."

"Sweetness, what about your knee?"

"I got a solution for that." Yes, her knee had severe bruising. Bruises and scrapes covered her entire body after her wipeout. All the more reason for her to be on top. She guided him to lay on the edge of the bed, and her bad knee went over the side. The better knee went over his hips, with his cock standing straight up at her, and they both groaned as she lowered herself over him. She leaned backward, keeping her arms away from his injured chest, and giving him quite the show.

The dazed look in his eyes filled her with satisfaction. His long fingers caressed her hips. Slowly, she rocked back and forth, grinding her clit on his pubic bone.

Pleasure started to build in her, and then she got bolder. Faster. Using her arms for leverage, she started lifting and lowering her pussy over his dick. Then his hands tightened their grip, and he started helping her lift, then thrusting his hips up as he brought her back down.

Frankie's eyes rolled back in her head, and she couldn't stop the cries of ecstasy every time he hit that spot inside her. And he did, every thrust, *hard.*

Soon, the telltale clenching in her core told her she was close. And then he brought her over the brink and followed right after, filling her with warmth.

Her bones felt like jelly as she rolled off him. Sam stood on shaky legs and fetched a washcloth from the bathroom and cleaned them both off. Then he took the washcloth back into the bathroom and returned with her satin sleep bonnet.

"I thought you might want this."

She sat up with a groan and a smile to take it from him. "Thank you." Once her hair had been tucked away, he followed her under the covers and wrapped his arms around her.

"I really am sorry, sweetness."

"I'm sorry, too. We shouldn't have kept it from you."

She felt and heard him sigh. "No, you should have. In the beginning, before I got to know you and Jenna, I would have turned you in. Now I think I found a way to have our cake and eat it, too."

Frankie chuckled. "I told myself not to do this because you worked for the government. I didn't want to put either of us in that position. But I couldn't help it."

"Put us in what position?"

She groaned. "You're going to make me say it, aren't you?"

"What's wrong with that?"

"You're not supposed to say it this soon after sex!"

He dragged a finger under her chin and raised it to look into her eyes. "Say what, Francesca?"

Those clear blue orbs seemed to drain all the sense from her. His gaze held so much understanding, so much emotion. It dragged out the words she hadn't wanted to say yet. "I... I love you."

She had always been guarded and closed off, keeping her emotions tightly locked away. But then she met him, and everything changed. He was different, someone who made her feel things she had never experienced before. The way he looked at her with such tenderness, the way he challenged her, and the way he understood her without her having to say a word. It was as if he had unlocked a part of her heart that had long been dormant. Getting attached to anyone, even friends, had never been a smart idea, having to move around so much. For the first time in her life, she found herself falling in love, and it was a feeling that consumed her completely.

He claimed her lips in response, cupping her face to hold her still for his tongue. Just as she thought she'd be ready for another round, he pulled back. "I love you, too, Frankie."

She smiled and snuggled into his chest. "Good. Then let me sleep."

Her head bounced in time with his chuckling. "Good night, Francesca."

"'Night, Sam."

Morning brought a gloomy sky and threats of storms. It fit her mood, as Frankie could feel every one of her aches and pains with intense clarity.

Grunting, she rolled herself up and sat on the bed to test her knee. It seemed to be okay to hold her weight again. She stood slowly, holding onto the nightstand until she was sure it would hold.

"Good morning," Sam grunted from the bed.

"Morning, soldier boy." Turning, she made her way slowly but surely toward the bathroom.

She took care of business and brushed her teeth. Sam knocked, and she opened the door. "Want me to leave?"

"I just wanted to see my chest."

"It's a lovely chest. Shame you had to mark it up last night."

"Believe me, it was not my idea." He stood naked in front of the mirror, taking in the incredible purple bruise that took up half his chest.

Frankie blinked as her eyes prickled. God, she could have lost him before they had the chance to make up.

"I'm super grateful for Kevlar right now."

"You and me both, sweetness." She rinsed her mouth, and he leaned over and kissed her cheek. "Alright, my turn."

"All yours, babe." She slipped into her room and shut the door behind her. "And we'll bring your stuff in here later and wash your sheets."

"Yup."

Minding her scrapes, Frankie dressed slowly. She picked out a soft pair of leggings and a sloppy old t-shirt that was worn to perfection. Pulling her bonnet off, she headed down the stairs to find some fucking pain reliever.

In the kitchen, she found Josie, Jenna, and Roger sitting around an open box of doughnuts.

"Hey girlie, how you feeling?" Jenna asked.

"A bit like I got run over by a truck," she admitted, pulling out the little white bottle and pouring herself a glass of water. "But my knee feels better."

"You look like you're walking better."

"What happened?" Josie asked, taking a sip of her juice.

"Some of our friends from the syndicate ran me off the road on my motorcycle yesterday. At least, that's who I think it was." Frankie swallowed her pills and chugged her water. When she saw Josie's wide stare, she waved her off. "I'm okay. I got off the bike in time and got home. Right now, I feel like a walking, talking bruise."

"I'm glad you're okay." Josie's voice seemed stronger than last night. And her skin wasn't as sallow.

"What did the hospital say?" She slid into a chair and poured herself some juice. Then she bit into a chocolate iced doughnut from the box. Mmm. Heaven.

"They said I have a concussion, and they gave me fluids for the dehydration."

"Did you tell them what happened?"

"Yes." Josie bit her lip. "Jenna said we have a contact at the FBI I'll probably have to speak to."

"Yeah. Sam works for them, but this isn't his area, so his friend is going to take the lead on the investigation." Roger explained.

"His name is Ross Patterson. I'll text him later this morning." Sam said as he entered the kitchen. "Dough-nuts?"

"We fucking earned them, brother. None of the three of us have been to bed yet."

Sam raised his eyebrows but said nothing as he pulled out a jelly-filled delight covered in powdered sugar. "I think I'm going to give the gym a break for a day or two."

"Same here." Roger shook his head.

"You guys need a nap. Jenna, do you have a spare set of sheets? I wanted to wash mine before I give the bed up for Josie."

Josie looked appalled. "Oh, you don't have to do that!"

"Frankie and I have been sharing a room, anyway. I can get us a hotel for the rest of my stay here if the air mattress doesn't work out."

She laid a hand on Josie's arm. "Please take it. I'd feel awful if you didn't."

"If... if you're sure." Josie blinked watery eyes. "Thank you."

Jenna pointed at Frankie. "Upstairs linen closet, third shelf down. And the washer and dryer are in the basement laundry room. It's the door off the gym." She laid her head in her hand. "If you can switch it, I'd appreciate it. I'm beat."

"I got a full night's sleep. Let me do this, Foxy." Frankie licked the frosting from her fingers and drank the rest of her juice. "I'll go get started."

"I'll be up to help you and move my shit."

She threw a thumbs up behind her and walked up the stairs. The more she moved, the better she felt.

Frankie found another set of sheets right where Jenna had told her they'd be. She carried them into the guest room and sat them on the dresser, then started pulling the sheets and pillowcases off the bed. When Sam got there, he helped her make the bed, then carried the dirty set down to the basement because, "My knees don't hurt."

Damn, a man that did laundry was sexy.

She fluffed the pillows and made sure the blanket was straight. Peeking in the closet, she saw he had clothes hung up there and carried them through the bathroom into her room. Well, their room, for now.

When Sam returned, he pulled things out of the dresser drawers and shoved them into his suitcase. Which he then carried into the other guest room. Next came a few miscellaneous items, like a cell phone and charger.

He deposited everything in the spare room she'd been occupying. "That's everything."

"I'll let Josie know she can get some sleep. Then maybe we can have that talk you wanted."

He smiled at her and tucked a strand of hair behind her ear. "I said everything I needed to say last night after you fucked my brains out. I love you, Frankie."

Her cheeks heated, and she grinned back at him. "I love you, too, Sam. And I've never said that to anyone before."

"I'm honored to be the first." Leaning over, he tried to kiss her gently, but she pressed herself against him and slipped him her tongue. She moaned when he pulled away. "We can still talk about where we go from here, sweetness."

Frankie pouted in jest. "Fine. I have to wait for the painkiller to kick in before I do anything fun, anyway."

"Alright, little hacker, let's go tell Josie her room is ready."

Frankie hobbled a bit down the stairs, leaning on the railing for support. Going up the stairs must have been easier than she'd realized, and she wondered how old people did anything if this was how it felt.

"Josie, you're all set upstairs." She gestured to the bedroom above.

"I'll show you which one is yours," Jenna said as she rose. Josie followed, the pair looking absolutely bushed.

"Sleep well, girls. I'll be up in a bit, Jenna." Instead of following them upstairs, Roger pulled out his phone.

"Aren't you exhausted?"

"Yeah. But I need to call Jon after I saw the news last night."

"What happened?" Sam asked, but he was already dialing. He did put it on speaker when Jon picked up.

"Hunt speaking."

"Jon, it's Roger."

"Roger? What's wrong?"

"I'm hoping you can tell me." Roger licked his lips, and Sam saw the tremor in his hand as he held out the phone. "I was sitting with a friend in the ER last night, and while I was in the waiting room, the CNN ticker announced that a roadside bomb had killed two soldiers in Afghanistan and wounded two others. Please... please tell me it's not Finn."

A deep inhale came over the line. Sam didn't know Jon the way he knew Roger, but he knew the sound of someone whose hands were tied. "I haven't heard anything, Rog. The news uses 'soldier' for everything. It's probably nothing."

"Keep your ear to the ground for me, will you? If Mom hears about this, she'll want to know."

"If it *is* him, they'll call her before anyone else."

Roger scrubbed a hand over his face, clearly not happy with his brother's lack of information. Frankie grimaced. She couldn't really relate not having any siblings, but she felt bad for Roger's obvious worry.

"I'll keep an eye out. I promise."

"Thanks."

"I'll talk to you later."

"Bye for now."

He hung up with a lost look on his face Frankie had never seen before.

"I just... I have a bad feeling."

"It's probably the lack of sleep," Sam offered. "Why don't you get upstairs and get a nap in? I'll call Ross and ask him to meet us tomorrow."

"Yeah, that sounds good." Roger cracked a yawn on the last word, then rose from the bar stool at the island and headed for the stairs. "Oh, before I forget," he turned around. "Nadia and Caleb's engagement party is Saturday. We're all invited."

Seriously? She'd met the chick once. But hey, free food, right?

"Let's talk about it after you wake up." Sam waved him up the stairs. Roger gave him a thumbs up and headed to bed.

They watched him go in silence. Once he was out of earshot, Frankie turned to Sam. "Do you think he'll be okay? His brother?"

Sam shrugged. "It takes days for the military to disseminate information. And with things like this, no news is good news."

Nodding, Frankie settled herself down on the couch and picked the remote up off the coffee table. "Wanna watch something?"

"I was going to hunt for apartments on my phone."

"Apartments."

"Yeah. Do you want to look with me?"

Frankie didn't realize she was tugging at her hair until he pulled a piece gently from between her fingers. She still wasn't used to this straight hair business. The stylist had said it would last for a week or two. "It's okay if you're not ready."

She sighed and leaned her head back, closing her eyes. "It's not that I don't *want* to, it's just..." He waited patiently for her to finish. Thankful for the space to process her thoughts, she ended up spewing them all out at once.

"I haven't shared space since the group home. I don't trust people not to eat my food, use my toothpaste, whatever. But in a relationship, you're supposed to share all that, anyway. I think that's how it works. Is it?" She opened her eyes to see Sam shrugging at her.

"I think it's whatever you want it to be. My parents didn't worry about all that, because they shared finances. And often they used the same things so it didn't make sense to have two of the same toothpaste. But if there's something specific you want for a snack, I don't need to eat any of it. Or if it's something I don't like, then it won't matter. It all comes down to communication. If you say, 'don't eat my fudge,' I'm not going to sneak down in the middle of the night and scarf it down. By the same token, if you don't tell me not to eat something and it's gone when you go for it, you can't be mad at me because I had no idea."

Frankie hummed as she considered his words. "Makes sense," she said. "I wasn't planning to share a bank account, though."

He shrugged. "No problem. We can split the bills down the middle. There are plenty of apps these days to make that easier."

"True. But we need an office space, so we're going to need at least two bedrooms."

"That's what I figured, too. I might be working in Roger's office here, though, so it might not be that bad."

"Hmm." She looked over his shoulder at the complex he'd pulled up on his phone. "Oh wow. That one's nice."

"I still have to talk to Roger about salary, but I have a savings account."

Frankie shook her head. "If you want to bring your furniture and everything, you'll need that to fund the move."

"True. What about you?"

She glanced down and pulled at a string hanging off her pants. "I brought everything with me that was mine." She'd always kept her possessions to a minimum. All those abrupt disruptions to her life had made her wary, and quick to run. For the first time, Frankie had a chance to set down roots in a place. It was... weird.

After living in the moment for so long, she wanted to make plans. A parade of images marched through her head. Friendsgiving at Jenna and Roger's house. Shopping for Christmas presents with Sam. Seeing snow for the first time in her life.

Her heart cracked wide open as she realized she could have this. That she deserved to make plans with people she cared about. They wanted a future with her.

She didn't realize she was crying until Sam reached over to thumb a tear away. "What's wrong, sweetness? What did I say?"

Shaking her head, Frankie wiped her cheeks, looking for more runaways, and sniffed. "Nothing. I'm... I'm just happy." She snorted as more tears fell. "God, I can't believe I'm that bitch now. Crying because I'm... I feel wanted for the first time ever."

Sam placed the phone down on the coffee table and opened his arms. Frankie leaned into him and reveled in the warm, safe feelings she got being in his arms. He didn't have to say anything. He just held her and let her get saline and snot on his old Army t-shirt as she released the pain she'd carried with her since birth.

Chapter 27

The following day, Ross met them at the public library in Hamburg, Maryland. That was the hometown he'd mentioned, a small town about an hour's drive from Baltimore.

He greeted Sam with a manly one-armed hug and slapped him on the back. "Great to see you, Sam. What did you find out?"

"Off the record?"

Ross shrugged. "Sure, if you want."

Sam released a breath he hadn't realized he'd been holding. "This might take some creative paperwork to keep my girlfriend out of jail."

His work acquaintance furrowed his brows. "How serious are we talking?"

"She used to work for them but wanted out when she realized what they were doing. And she went to her friend who also had left the organization, although she didn't know the extent of the trouble then."

Ross rubbed his chin. "That should come under whistle blower laws. I'll make sure nothing happens to them."

"Thanks." Sam offered his hand, and Ross shook it. Then he gestured Sam to the conference table.

"Take a seat. Tell me everything."

When Sam had finished the story, Ross's eyes were wide, but he showed no other signs of surprise. Sam had a reputation for being straight-laced and by the book, so he was sure this seemed out of character for him.

"I'm going to need a lot of statements."

"Frankie changed the code on the house so they can't get in and remove evidence. She'll give the code to you so you can send in a team once you get the warrant."

"If I can get a statement from the victim you rescued, I guarantee the judge will give us one."

"Let me call them in." Sam stood to return to the main section of the library.

"Shit, they're here with you?"

He turned to face Ross, whose eyebrows had disappeared into his hairline. "We only wanted to do this once."

Ross lifted a briefcase from the floor and opened it. "I'll get the forms ready."

Sam slipped into the hallway and strode back to the main library. Roger and Jenna were perusing the crime section. Josie watched the children's story hour, and Frankie was surfing the internet.

"Hey," he murmured, tapping her on the shoulder. "Ross wants to talk to everyone." She nodded, logged out, and followed as he gathered the others.

They followed him back to the conference room, where Ross waited with a pen, a recorder, and a pile of paperwork.

Sam made the introductions, then let Ross take the floor.

"Okay, I'm going to just get everyone's story from the beginning of when they got caught up in the syndicate until the night you found Josie. I'm guessing you gentlemen only got caught up because of your girls."

Roger made the so-so gesture with his hand. "There's a police report in Florida about the time they kidnapped me. I have the precinct and number for you if you need it."

"Great. Sam?"

"I've been in this the shortest amount of time."

"Get comfy. By the way, there's a fantastic diner down the street. We can all go get dinner when we're done and you can meet my future wife."

It was Sam's turn to be surprised. "I didn't know you were engaged."

Ross waved him off. "We're not yet, but it's going to happen."

Sam snorted. "Cocky bastard."

Ross gave him a sly smile and a shrug, then sat down and motioned for the rest of them to sit. One by one, he talked to the women and recorded their stories of how the syndicate got their claws in them.

When he got to Josie, the girls both slid their chairs closer to her. Hers was the hardest story to listen to.

Then when they got to the night they rescued Josie, the four of them told the story together, each filling in different parts. Sam forwarded him the video and photos he'd taken of the customer, and the man he'd taken with him.

Once everything was done and recorded, Ross addressed the group. "This is what I recommend. You two," he pointed at Jenna and Frankie, "are technically whistle blowers. That grants you immunity. All three of you could go into witness protection." The girls shook their heads. Ross turned and looked directly at Josie. "Are you sure?"

Josie bit her swollen lip and wiped more tears from her face. "I don't want to get passed around to strangers. It's enough these nice people have taken me in. I barely even recognize myself anymore. I just want to heal. They stole my whole life." When she started to cry again, Frankie slipped an arm around her, and she leaned in.

Ross gave her a look of sympathy. "Alright. Then I recommend you all lie low for a while. Maybe go visit some relatives. I'll keep in touch with Sam and let you know when we make our move to arrest the syndicate. Roger, I think Josie needs to stay with you and Jenna. She trusts you, and you have the skills to protect her if they come after her."

"They won't. They probably left me for dead." Josie's voice held no inflection.

"Josie?" Ross spoke gently. She raised her head to look at him. "If you end up on any kind of media before we get these guys, they will find out they were wrong. And they'll come after you because you can identify them. Speaking of which, I'll need to meet with you again once we have them in custody, so you can pick them out of a lineup."

Josie trembled, but she agreed.

"Thank you so much for coming forward, folks. Sam, I'll get with your contacts in the Denver office so we can combine the cases." Ross tucked his papers away and shut his briefcase. "Now let's go to the diner and get some food. I'm starving and Heather should get off work…" he checked his watch. "In about ten minutes."

"I'm going to go to the girls' room first." Josie stood with Frankie and Jenna flanking her.

"That sounds like a great idea. Let's go." Sam smiled at his little hacker as she and Jenna escorted Josie out of the room.

JOSIE GAZED AROUND THE backyard once more, in awe of how many people were here. This engagement party was her first real social event since her rescue, and Roger had promised all these people were safe. The number of friends and family here to wish his little sister and her fiancé well overwhelmed her. So she'd holed herself up in a chair on the back porch, next to a small heater.

Nadia wasn't much younger than her, and she'd been gracious when Roger and Jenna brought her along, welcoming Josie to this party herself. Thanks to the unseasonably warm fall day, a pickup football game had started in the side yard, between shirts and skins. They'd piled leaves up into makeshift goal posts. Roger had gone to play, and

Jenna was grabbing food, so Sam stayed close to her. They treated her security with the utmost care, but she never felt like she was being babysat.

She remembered this used to feel normal. Would she ever get back there?

Frankie and Jenna returned with food for themselves and a plate for Sam. "Here, babe."

"Thanks, Frankie." Sam bit into his burger and groaned. "That hits the spot."

Jenna looked at her half-eaten plate. "Did you want anything else, Josie?"

Josie shook her head and took a sip of her Coke. Her stomach was so tiny. She'd found herself eating small snacks whenever she felt the urge. After so long being under the syndicate's control and only being allowed one tiny meal a day, she wondered if it would ever return.

Usually, she only drank water. As a nurse, she was hyperaware of how dehydrated she'd been and part of her still feared that basic necessity being taken away. Not that she was doing any nursing at the moment. To earn her keep, she'd started cleaning Roger's house. Before Josie had even met Nadia, Jenna had contacted her to see if any of her friends had clothes she could wear. She was completely reliant on these people's kindness, and it grated on her. But they didn't ask her to do anything. Just heal. It was ... it was enough to start restoring her faith in humanity. Just a little.

As far as nursing went, she'd have to get licensed for Maryland, anyway. Ugh, would she have to study for her boards again? Time was still an odd construct for her to think about.

A whistle cut through the yard, and the roar of the game suddenly died down. One of the bridesmaids, as indicated by her sash, stood next to a guy who was taking his fingers out of his mouth.

"Thanks, Jake." The blonde smiled up at him. "Mrs. Hunt, the house phone is ringing!" She waved a cordless phone up in the air, and Judy strode across the yard to grab it.

"Hello? This is she." Then Mrs. Hunt went white as a ghost and Jake was catching her before she could fall over. Irving, Roger, and Jon noticed, and all raced to her side.

"I — I understand. Yes, thank you." She hung up the phone and flung herself into her husband's arms.

"Judy? Who was it? What's wrong?"

As if realizing that she still had guests, Judy drew herself up, though she still clutched onto him for dear life. "It... it's Finn. He's been... wounded."

Nadia cried out and buried her face in Caleb's chest.

Josie's heart broke for Roger's family. He'd mentioned a brother on a deployment that first morning after the hospital, but they hadn't had many chances to talk about him.

She continued, her voice shaking. "We need to go to Germany. They... couldn't tell me anything else. We have to get to the base in Germany."

Irving was nodding, gripping her elbows as if he were also just trying to keep from falling apart. "Then that's what we'll do. I'll get the passports and the suitcases."

Judy was already nodding, then turned and took her sobbing daughter's face in her hands. "He's alive. We'll bring him home, okay?" Mother and daughter hugged, then she turned Nadia back to Caleb.

"The party doesn't have to be over. You all can stay. Nadia knows how to lock the house up. Nadia, have people take the food from the party home. One of you three, take any fruit or milk in the fridge home with you. I don't know how long we'll be." She turned to Roger and Jon. "You two, make sure the trash is out, and the mail doesn't pile up, okay?" They nodded and hugged her in turn.

But the festive mood had broken in a single sentence. The four girls wearing bridesmaid sashes gathered around Nadia and Caleb in a group hug. By the time Judy and Irving emerged, someone produced a bunch of takeout containers and divided the food up among everyone. With so many people helping, clean up took no time at all.

Josie left with Roger and Jenna back to their place. She watched Roger from the back seat in silence, holding the container of diamond ring-shaped cookies in her lap. Having lived through her own insane plot twist, she knew without a doubt the Hunt family would never be the same.

Epilogue

December

Sam had to hold back his whistle as he strolled through the familiar, bland hallways of the Bureau building. He had his resignation letter in his hand and he was ready to get out of there.

Lachlan wasn't going to be happy, but he couldn't bring himself to care. The only good thing about Lachlan's demands for organization and cleanliness meant that Sam's office was already labeled for the archives guys. He'd packed his few personal possessions into his empty lunch bag and left it in the office.

His boss's only nod to the impending holiday season was a scraggly little pre-decorated tree on his desk. Sam suspected the kids had bought it for him one year. Unfortunately for the rest of the team, Lachlan's mood was decidedly Grinch-y.

"Ivers! It's been a hell of a month. You ready to get back to work?" Lachlan didn't wait for an answer before turning around and rustling through the filing cabinet next to his desk. "I got a case with your name on it."

"I don't think that's wise, sir," Sam responded. "I am resigning and it seems like poor planning to take on another assignment when I'll just have to hand it off."

The folder slipped out of Lachlan's hand, spilling all over his carefully organized drawer. But Lachlan didn't move to clean it up. He just stared at Sam, his mouth gaping open. Sam laid his letter in the middle of Lachlan's desk. "I've already forwarded it to HR and they're sending the tech guy down to verify my equipment's all here."

It was the first time Sam had ever seen Lachlan speechless. He stammered, and Sam waited patiently for him to find his words.

"Just like that? No notice?"

"I have another job waiting for me and I have to pack up my entire apartment to get to it. I'm leaving Denver." He probably shouldn't have said that much. It wasn't any of Lachlan's business where Sam went.

Hayden from I.T. was waiting in the office, his FBI-issued laptop bag open and his equipment spread out over the desk.

"Everything checks out, Sam. I wish you luck." Hayden reached out to shake Sam's hand. Sam hadn't had a reason to call the I.T. office many times throughout his time at the FBI, but he always treated his fellow computer nerds with respect.

"I wish you luck as well," he responded, then he took his lunch bag and headed for the security desk, where he turned in his badge and left for the last time.

Walking back to his Jeep, a final weight lifted from Sam's chest. He took a deep breath as a free man, and grinned. Tossing his bag into the passenger seat, he headed for home, where his Francesca was supposedly helping him pack.

FRANKIE HAD INTENDED TO start Sam's packing while he went into the office and submitted his resignation. Really, she had. But the man had so many *books*. The amount of stuff one single guy had accumulated had astounded her as someone who made sure to accumulate very little. She'd spent an hour or so taping boxes together, and she'd even filled two, but then she got to his thrillers and saw one that she had to read the back of. Which then turned into opening said book and reading the first few pages, just to see if it was as good as she'd heard. *That* had turned into curling up on his couch and getting so lost in her reading that she didn't hear the key turn in the lock. So when he stood over and said, "Packing is going well, I see," she gave a small shriek and clasped the book to her chest.

"Holy shit, you scared me."

Sam grinned. "You were worlds away."

"True."

He produced a bookmark from a shelf she hadn't gotten to yet and placed it between the pages. "Let's keep that one out of the boxes for now. You can read it on the way to Baltimore."

"I'll probably finish it before we're done packing." Frankie carefully laid it on the coffee table while Sam just shrugged.

One look at the clock told her it wasn't even close to lunch time yet. "That didn't take long."

"Nope." Sam sat down on the couch and kicked his feet up. "Feels good to get out of there."

"I know what you mean." And she did. The freedom she'd felt erasing her data from the syndicate's servers had been dampened by the knowledge of what they'd done, but it had still been there.

"What are you going to do about your bike?"

They'd avoided talking about that day, but since the apartment they had picked back in Baltimore only had one parking space, it made sense he'd ask. "Caleb gave me the number to a shop that specializes in bodywork. They do more custom builds, but for actual repair he said I should take it to his friends from vo-tech."

"What did they say?"

She sighed. "Well, I haven't had a chance to take it over yet, but they said from what I told them, it's going to cost a few thousand, easy." She shrugged. "There's no point taking it to them until January anyway. They're booked for the rest of the year."

"You'll have the money by then."

"How?" She was still confused as to how she was supposed to leverage her hacker skills to make money without stealing.

"It's easy. You and I are going to be working for Roger."

Frankie tilted her head. "Really?"

"Yeah. Businesses will hire us to hack into their systems and tell them their weaknesses."

"They're gonna pay us to hack them?" This sounded too good to be true.

"Yeah, it's something companies do all the time. And with all the black hat hackers out there, there's a huge market for it."

He must have seen the naughty thoughts starting to circulate, because he caught her chin and looked right into her eyes. "You're getting paid to do it so you can't steal anything."

She whined, just to tease him. "But it's right there!"

"And it's not yours."

They grinned at each other. Her ingrained habits would be hard to break, but Frankie was determined to live a life she wouldn't have to hide. And if she wanted to keep her white hat hacker, she'd have to become one, as well.

But she could tease him about it a little.

"Do I have to spank you?"

Her eyes shifted back and forth even as she fought the laugh. "No."

"Later, little hacker." He stood and offered her his hand. "First, let's get some boxes packed. I have the storage pod coming tomorrow, so we can start loading it up."

"When did you want to get back to Baltimore?"

"Well, our lease just started and this one ends at the end of the month. So I'd like to spend Christmas with the

Hunts." Sam blew a breath out. "Roger hasn't told me any news about his brother yet, but I think they're going to need all the support they can get."

Frankie nodded. "According to the tips I saw on the internet, we should pack up things that you don't use on a regular basis first."

"That's why you were packing the books." Sam nodded. "Good call. I'll help. These things can get heavy."

As they separated Sam's things into piles to pack and to donate, Frankie no longer felt overwhelmed by all the things he had. They were just that: things. And Sam made it clear that she was far more important than any of them.

They took a pile of books to the used bookstore, and then a box of movies and old video games he'd beaten to the game exchange. With the cash he got, he took her to dinner. Nothing fancy, just the burger joint at the mall, but it was nice to go on a date for once. After the hookups she'd relied on for scratching the physical itch, this filled a void Frankie hadn't even noticed was missing.

During dinner, Sam licked his lips, then asked her a question she'd run from before. "I'm planning on visiting my mom in the spring. Do you want to come along?"

He wanted to introduce her to his mom, and Frankie found that no longer scared her. She could put down roots. She could make plans. And Sam wouldn't take them away. She didn't have to keep running.

She smiled at him as she answered. "Yes, I do."

Thank you so much for reading Hacker's Accomplice!
Don't forget to leave a review!

Can you guess who's next? Survivor's Sniper is coming
December 1st!

Also By Jasmine

For a current list of my available titles, scan the QR code below:

Notes from Jasmine

Thank you so much for reading Frankie and Sam's story! They really took me by surprise while I was writing Thief's Bodyguard. I had intended for this series to be only about the Hunt brothers but Eraser X, though, would not stay in the background. And I love her for it. It turned out Frankie and Sam were just too good a story to pass up. Plus, it made more sense to give them their own book when it was clear Frankie would be instrumental in the overarching plot against the syndicate.

Thank you Maria, for clearing up the process for injury notifications, and for all your guidance and advice. To my beta team, thank you for reading so quickly when I realized how little time I gave myself. Jayla, you were phenomenal at bringing Frankie to life on the page and I appreciate you giving me a window into your culture. Jenn, thank you for being the best editor and being willing to push me to make these books the best I can. Thank you Sarah

Kil, for the amazing cover that looked so perfect despite having to make our own blond model (haha!) Thanks to Jenna Moreci, Sasha Black, and Abbie Emmons for the YouTube videos. And last but not least, Dale. L. Roberts, for fostering a wonderful community of indie authors.

XOXO,

Jasmine

About the Author

I inherited my love of reading from my parents. As the daughter of two teachers, one of whom is also a librarian, I was the kid who walked out of the library with the maximum number of books each week, then walked back in the following week having read every single one. This would go on all summer long. When I could put pencil to paper, I started writing my own (terrible) kid's stories. Around age eight, I told my mom I wanted to be an author when I grew up, but she talked me out of it. She wanted me to have a stable career because of my poor health.

While I learned to manage my chronic condition through childhood, I also kept writing as a creative outlet. But when I grew up and turned my focus to my career, writing went by the wayside. The stories would not come again until quarantine in 2020 when trauma from the year before poured out of me in a cathartic story now known as *Roar for Me*. The decision to self-publish was an easy one. I consider each book its own work of art and I want to control not only what I write, but all the packaging, as well.

I write books I want to read. This means intelligent characters, happy-ever-afters, and no cheating. Adult contemporary romances with plenty of steam appeal to me the most. Music and pop culture are my biggest sources of inspiration. And I love to flip the script and surprise readers by putting a twist on their expectations.

Everyone deserves their own love story. I've always believed that. I want to develop a wide range of characters so everyone can relate to someone in one of my books. I especially love challenging gender expectations. And I hope my books will be an escape for readers, not just entertainment. When I'm not writing, I'm working in healthcare in my native Pittsburgh. Or you might find me crafting, baking sweet treats, or playing *Mario Kart* with my own nerdy love.

www.ingramcontent.com/pod-product-compliance
Lightning Source LLC
Chambersburg PA
CBHW032147050726
47591CB00001B/115